Making A Texas Cowboy

Making A Texas Cowboy

A *Home At Last Texas* Romance

Justine Davis

TULE
PUBLISHING

Dedication

This one is for the entire incredible, amazing, caring Tule team.

They're the reason I came back to Last Stand.

Chapter One

T HEY'D MADE IT nearly an hour this time before somebody recognized him.

Jackson Thorpe let out a suppressed sigh as he watched his son, Jeremy, playing in the sand. Well, not exactly playing, although there were toys beside him. The seven-year-old spent more time simply grabbing fistfuls of sand and letting them spill out through his fingers.

Watching life slip away . . .

He couldn't seem to rid his mind of the thought he'd had the first time he'd seen Jeremy endlessly watching those grains of sand slip out of his grasp.

Bringing the boy to the beach on this New Year's Day had been a desperate grab for something, anything that would give him hope things would improve. Jeremy had always loved the beach, so much that his mother brought him here every chance she got. And he'd hoped that the winter holiday would mean fewer people there. No such luck.

But then his luck had run out two years ago.

He bit his lip, hard, trying to stop the stinging tears that wanted to form.

Leah, I don't know what to do.

God, he missed her. Missed her smile, her laugh, that wisdom that had been so amazing for a woman still in her twenties. He had a couple of years on her, and was nowhere near as smart about people, especially their son. She was the same in his thoughts as she'd been then, teasing him about being an old man at thirty. She was frozen in his mind, just as she'd been at twenty-nine.

Because she never saw thirty.

"Jackson!"

"Mr. Thorpe!"

"It's Austin Holt!"

He smothered a sigh at that last shout of the too-familiar name from the growing cluster of people, some paparazzi, some apparent fans, some just beachgoers wondering what the fuss was, trying to clamber over the rocks to get to them. Every beach in California was technically public up to the mean high tide line, but this little one in front of Miles Flint's place was exceptionally hard to get to under that rule, protected by the rocks that jutted far out into the water on one side, and a cliff with a sheer drop of over fifty feet on the other. Because of that, many of his friends—including the star of his latest television series that had become one of those soaring, engulfing things that had taken over most of the country—used it. Because his friends were the kind of people who treasured what was hardest for them to get: privacy.

You've hit the big time, Jackson, and now you're going to see the downside. You won't be able to sneeze without somebody getting it on video and spreading it far and wide, usually with lies attached.

He'd thought Miles was exaggerating, at the time. But the successful producer had been generous with his offer to come here anytime, and Jackson had gladly taken him up on it, for his family's sake. Of course, the fact that *Stonewall* had paid for a big chunk of this piece of high-end real estate probably made it an equitable trade. Miles had taken the chance of casting an unknown with no real experience in a modern-day western, and it had paid off a thousandfold when the show had shattered just about every broadcast and streaming record there was. Miles—and he, himself—had been riding high on the kind of wave only hitting the zeitgeist of the culture at the right time with the right story could create. They had—

"Is that Jeremy?"

The shout in a shrill female voice jolted him out of his reverie. That was it. The recognition of him was one thing, and part of the job. He'd always thought those who pretended not to want it, even as they made sure they got it, were the worst sort of phony. But when it came to his son, especially now, every considerable protective instinct he had kicked into overdrive at the slightest hint of intrusion into the boy's seemingly bottomless grief.

He didn't wait for the boy to get up and walk back to the

house with him. He simply picked him up and took him. And tried not to wince at how light he was. He should weigh about fifty pounds by now, and Jackson knew he didn't. Knew he'd lost weight when he should be gaining it rapidly. But every meal was a battle, albeit a very quiet one. Because just like now, when he'd picked him up, Jeremy didn't fight, didn't argue, didn't pitch a fit. He just sat there and wouldn't eat. Even things he'd gobbled down like a starving dog before.

He put the boy down once they were inside. Watched as his son sat on the couch, not the one facing the wall of windows looking out at the water, but on the one facing the fireplace wall, with the big painting of the place that had inspired *Stonewall.* The sprawling hills covered with blue-bonnets in full bloom was a bright, colorful thing, although Jackson knew the color was transitory because the flowers only lasted about a month.

Miles had told him he'd had the painting for a couple of years before the idea of telling a story about it had occurred to him. He'd often talked about it in interviews. Which had been frequent after he'd become the hottest creator in Hollywood when the show had blasted through the summer doldrums to become the biggest thing going five years ago. Carrying Jackson along with it, taking him from a guy wrangling horses and scrounging for bit parts, to the flavor of the month. That month had become a year, that year two, then more, until he'd grown sick of seeing his own face everywhere.

Before he'd lost the only anchor that had kept him sane and grounded. Before the accident that had ended the life they'd built, the only life his son had ever known. The son who now sat in what had become his usual silence, just staring at the painting he wasn't even sure the boy was seeing at all.

With an effort that never seemed to get any easier, he pulled his mind out of that ugly rut. He went to the kitchen and grabbed a couple of the candy bars Jeremy had always loved, figuring at least there were nuts in it that would provide some nutrition. He walked back to the living room and sat beside him on the couch. He tossed one of the bars at his son and proceeded to unwrap the other himself, hoping the boy would just follow suit. He took a bite, making himself look at the painting and not Jeremy. It did taste good, although he didn't indulge often.

After a moment he heard the tearing of another wrapper, and he dared to hope it had worked.

"Funny how that painting inspired *Stonewall*," he said, still without looking at Jeremy. "Miles was just sitting here one night, just like we are, looking at it, and started asking himself questions about it. 'What ifs,' he called them. What if there was a ranch there, what if it was a family ranch, what if the guy who owned it had never expected to? What if, what if, what if?"

Jeremy said nothing, but Jackson caught out of the corner of his eye that the boy had taken a bite. He waited until he'd swallowed before trying to draw him into a conversation, an effort that was usually met with words of one syllable, or a shrug and no words at all.

He finally looked at his son. "What would you ask?"

He'd about resigned himself to the usual no answer when Jeremy said, very quietly, "What if it was real?"

Jackson froze. Five whole words. And an actual answer, not simply a variation on "Nothing," or "Leave me alone." It took him a moment of near-frantic thinking to decide how to respond. The only thing he was sure of was that it had to be normal, sound normal, as if this wasn't the first time since that awful day the boy had actually participated in a conversation.

"The place in the painting?" he asked, hoping more questions would keep it going.

"The ranch. I wish the ranch was real."

He was talking. He was actually talking. Jackson had to steady himself to go on. "The ranch . . . from the show?" Jeremy nodded. "You mean in Texas?" Another nod. Jackson held his breath for a moment before he finally asked, "Why?"

The boy shrugged, and Jackson resigned himself to the end of the conversation, but still counting it a win because the boy had actually communicated. But then Jeremy spoke again. "Because then we could go live there. For real. Not just you pretending."

Jackson had never felt this before, this sensation that everything, absolutely everything, depended on what he said next. A crucial scene where he had to deliver a killer line had never, ever mattered as much as this did.

"Well, that place"—he gestured at the painting—"is real. It doesn't always look like that, with the flowers, but it's real. In fact, it's not far from where your aunt Trista lives."

For the first time Jeremy turned to look at him. "It is?"

He nodded, since the boy was looking at him now. "In fact, I've been thinking we should go see her. She's really sad, missing your uncle David. You know how bad that feels. Maybe we could all make each other feel better."

"She still remembers him?"

It had been two years longer for Trista, but there wasn't a doubt in Jackson's mind she had adored her husband with everything in her. "Yes. She thinks about him every day."

Jeremy looked down, apparently fascinated by a bit of sand clinging to his knee. Finally, barely above a whisper, he asked, "Will I remember Mom?"

It was like a knife to the gut for Jackson. He had no idea this was bothering the boy. He slid off the couch and swung around to kneel in front of his son.

"You will never, ever forget her, Jeremy. It's just that someday you'll be able to think about her and it won't hurt as much as it does now."

"Does it hurt you?"

"More than anything in my life."

Except the thought that I'm losing you too.

He hoped that this, the most his son had spoken since the day he'd had to tell him Mom wasn't ever coming home, marked a turning point.

As it turned out, in a way, it had.

His son shut down even more. Completely.

And Jackson Thorpe, the man who pretended in front of cameras to be the guy with all the answers, the ruler of a small kingdom in the state that had once been its own country, had no answer for this.

HE WOKE WITH a start. Realized he was on the floor. Couldn't remember how he got there. He raised his head. Blinked, trying to see in the darkness of the room. When he recognized where he was, on the floor in the living room at home, in front of the couch, it all came rushing back. The waiting for the nosy ones to give up before putting Jeremy in the car and leaving Miles's place for home, although it didn't feel like that anymore. Getting there, and Jeremy assuming the same position he had at the beach, staring at seemingly nothing. Himself, determined to get the boy talking again, like he had in those moments in front of that painting.

Determined, and failing.

He sat up hurriedly, but carefully; he didn't want to make a noise that might wake the boy sleeping on the couch.

There had been a time when, waking up on the floor, he

would have assumed he'd passed out drunk. But no more. That month-long binge after Leah died was both the first and last of his life. Thanks to his sister, who had flown to California to confront him after his best friend, Tucker, had called her in concern. She'd arrived at the house to find him face down in the bathroom after having nearly puked his guts out. Knowing him all too well, she took video of the scene, then of Jeremy huddled in a corner of his room, saying he "tried to take care of Daddy," and finished it off with his own vicious rant as he woke up, realized she was there and what she was doing.

She'd made him watch the video, and when he looked into his son's eyes, saw how broken he looked, he knew he'd reached the end of this little experiment that hadn't worked, anyway. A few hours of oblivion was not worth that look on an already broken-hearted five-year-old's face. And he went back to his old habits, which involved nothing more than an occasional drink on special occasions.

He sat there silently, propped up against the coffee table, looking at the boy curled up in an almost fetal position, hands clenched even in sleep around the knitted blanket Jackson had put over him last night. The throw his mother had made for him, with the image of his favorite creature, a roadrunner, worked into it. He stared at the whimsical design, remembering how it was that very thing about Leah, her sense of whimsy, that had kept him sane and at least somewhat balanced when the rocket that was *Stonewall* had first taken off.

After Tris had brutally awakened him to the additional damage he was doing to an already devastated child, he'd done everything he could think of. He'd taken more time off to be with Jeremy, with the producers' understanding, even as it screwed up their schedule for the rest of the year. He'd found a doctor with a stellar reputation for dealing with bereavement in children and followed every suggestion the woman gave after her sessions with his son. Nothing had helped.

In a crazy way Jeremy's desperate state had muffled his own grief over losing Leah; he was so terrified he was going to lose their child, too, that he doubted his brain had fully processed the actual loss.

When he'd gone back to work, he'd frequently had the boy visit on the days they were filming exteriors because he seemed to like it when they were outside with the animals—cows, horses, and a couple of well-trained acting dogs. Jeremy had gone, but silently. He'd petted the horses, the dogs, even a calf or two. Then he'd hidden out in Jackson's trailer, refusing to come out, huddling on the bunk in the back so much like he'd been in that video that it made Jackson more than a little queasy.

Like he was huddled on the couch now.

He stared at the boy.

I wish the ranch was real.

He grabbed the phone he'd tossed on the chair he'd vacated to take this spot closer to his son. Glanced at the time. Five a.m. here. That would make it seven a.m. for Tris. Which would mean she'd probably been up for at least an hour, probably more. She hadn't slept well since David's death.

And you didn't understand . . . then.

But he did now. And so would Tris.

He stared unseeingly at the phone. He knew what would happen if he did this. He'd be screwing over the crew, which he hated. He'd be aggravating the producers, including Miles, but also Felix, which he hated a little less. The arrogant jerk deserved a bit of aggravation. He'd probably go after him legally, eventually, so there was that. He also might be killing the show altogether, and he didn't like that either.

But he loved his son.

He made the call.

Chapter Two

"**Y**OU DID WHAT?"

Finished pouring her own glass of wine, Trista offered him one, but he shook his head. "You put the fear of alcohol in me for good with that video."

"That was the plan," she said.

"Testing me?"

"Part of my job as the big sister."

She instead got him a bottle of sweet tea from the fridge and handed it over.

"Now," she said, "back to my question. You did what?"

He studied the bottle in his hands. "I walked out."

"Let me be clear on this. You quit the show?"

"That's up to them. I just told them I was leaving, and I didn't know when I'd be back."

"You walked away from the biggest television show in the country and half the world, the show that made you? That won you all those awards that clutter up your bookshelves?"

His head came up. "I thought you hated it."

"I hate how fake the Texas parts are," she corrected. "I

love your success. You deserve it, bro. You're really good."
She gave him a crooked grin. "I never really realized before
how good you were, until you had me forgetting you were
my brother, not this guy who doesn't exist."

He gave a half shrug. "He's a lot tougher than I am."

"But you make it believable." She studied him for a long,
silent moment before saying, "You know most of the world
will think you're crazy, walking away from a show that big."

He met her gaze, looked into her familiar, always loving
eyes. Eyes so like his own, the deep blue of their father. It
had been a standing mock argument in their family when
they were growing up, whether the eyes looked better with
his dark hair or her auburn. Each of them had always voted
for the other.

"I had to leave, Tris. I was losing Jeremy. He's more important than anything else."

Her eyes took on a sudden sheen, and she blinked rapidly a couple of times. "Yes. Yes, he is."

He knew she understood. She and David had not, sadly,
had any children, but she understood. "He makes it all both
better and worse, doesn't he?" she asked softly.

He remembered his own earlier thought. Leave it to his
brilliant sister to distill it down to the essence. "Yes."

She sipped at her wine, pushed a strand of hair that had
fallen forward behind her ear, then glanced toward the
hallway entrance. There, two doors down, his son slept—
hopefully—in the foldout cot in the room that usually served

as his sister's office. They'd had a discussion about this, and it had been Tris who'd suggested that instead of putting the boy on the sofa out here where he had usually slept when they visited—when Leah had been alive—they share the room.

"I just think he needs to know you won't leave him too," she'd said, giving him yet another glimpse into the mind of a kid who wasn't quite old enough to completely understand the concept of death. As a teacher, Tris had more than once dealt with a child in Jeremy's position.

Even as he thought it, she asked a very teacher-like question. "Pulling Jeremy out of school like that . . . aren't you afraid that will mess him up more?"

"I'm not sure he could be messed up more," he admitted.

"Then we've got a job ahead of us," she said, calmly.

Again, he felt the stirring of regret that she and David hadn't had children. Then felt bad for that feeling, because it would put his sister in the same shoes he was in, that of a person grieving their so very much loved spouse and striving to keep their equally beloved child from strangling in the clutches of their own grief. Even if he didn't fully understand it, Jeremy knew his mother was gone. And it had been Tris who had warned him that the boy might find a reason to blame himself, which was exactly what had happened. Jackson had spent a long, sad night holding his son and assuring him that him scaring his mom with his new sling-shot glider hadn't made her so mad at him, she'd left.

"How did you do it?" he asked bleakly. "How did you get past losing David?"

She set her glass down and stared at him. "What makes you think I have?"

He knew he'd made a big mistake. "I'm sorry, I didn't—"

"You think because I get up and go to work every day, I'm past it? You think because I'm functional, I'm past it? Well, stick around, brother mine, and you'll see what a mess I still am. If you hear me crying in the dark, ignore it. If you see me wearing his shirt, ignore it. If you—"

Jackson got to his feet and pulled his sister up out of her chair. He enveloped her in a hug, squeezing as tightly as he thought he could without actually hurting her.

"I'm an idiot, Tris. You already know that, but in case you'd forgotten, that was my latest reminder."

He felt her sigh against him, and finally she hugged him back. "I think it's in the brother's job description."

"Wish I wasn't so good at it."

He heard, muffled against his chest, the familiar laugh. "And that is why I love you, Jackson Thorpe. You've never let it all go to your head, when you easily could have."

"Maybe that's because I know damned well I just happened to be doing the right thing in the right place at the right time."

"Three rights don't make a wrong, you know."

He leaned back, gave her a wry grin. "Four rights. I forgot to add that it was in front of the right person."

"Some people would see that as meant to be."

"In my world, most would see it as sheer dumb luck."

"I know. One of the things I don't like about your world."

"One of the many," he said, knowing his sister did not have the highest opinion of his line of work.

She backed away far enough to give him the determined look he knew so well. "But I'm proud of you," she said with that Tris-like adamance that had been in her voice ever since he'd been old enough to understand when she was defending him.

"And I you, sis. You handled this much better than I have."

"You have Jeremy to worry about too. And like I said, I'm not past losing David any more than you're past losing Leah."

"We're a couple of miserable ones, aren't we?"

Her expression changed then, gentled. "But we had something many people are never lucky enough to have. Someone to love completely, and who loved us the same way."

He had to swallow, and it was tight, before he could get out a single word. "Yeah."

"Now," she said with that finality that warned him she was about to start organizing. "I think we should take a drive tomorrow, so Jeremy can see a bit of the countryside, then head into town for lunch and a walking tour of Last Stand."

He sighed. "As long as you know he's likely to not be interested. He hasn't been interested in anything. The shrink he was seeing said he'd never had a tougher case."

She looked thoughtful. "Perhaps he's starting to realize never means never."

"As in his mother's never coming back? Yeah, I think he is. He asked me the other day if he would forget her. The longest conversation we've had in months."

"Did you tell him he never would?"

"I did. But that's one reason we came. I thought he should be around someone who never has."

He'd never seen so much pain and love combined as he saw then in his sister's eyes. She and David had both fought his illness so hard, only to lose the battle seven years ago. Jackson knew how devastated she'd been at his death, and how hard she'd fought to simply keep going. She'd had every reason in the world to disconnect, but she never stopped trying to function.

He wasn't sure he had her grit. He wondered if he'd still be mired in this grief in five more years.

"I'm glad you came," Tris said. "Maybe I can make up a little for being so lost when he was born."

He didn't know what to say to that. So instead he hugged her again.

Chapter Three

"OH, MY GOD. Look, is that . . . who I think it is?"

Nicole Baylor swallowed her sip of Java Time's luscious latte before she turned to look in the direction her friend Jessica was staring. She saw a couple of locals, the barber and the woman who was the hostess at Valencia's restaurant, but neither of them would warrant Jess's stunned reaction.

The only other thing she saw was the not unusual knot of people a couple of blocks up, next to the statue in front of the library—the towering bronze figure of Asa Fuhrmann, the iconic hero of the actual last stand the town was named for. Even the abbreviated version of the man's actions that were written on the plaque on the base, about him making a run for more ammunition when the defenders were pinned down, a run that had cost him his life but saved the others, made for attention-grabbing reading.

Then, of course, there was the newer plaque just above the sizeable chunk taken out of the pedestal Asa stood on, explaining more heroics, this time of Police Chief Shane Highwater, who had pulled a survivor out of the flames of an engulfed vehicle that had been stopped from doing even more damage than killing two occupants only by the solid presence of that statue. Nicole had been here that April day, the day of town matriarch Minna Herdmann's birthday, when practically every resident of Last Stand showed up to honor the centenarian-plus, who amazingly was still with them and likely would be for the town celebration of her birthday again this year. Her hometown was full of fascinating—and when necessary, heroic—people.

"It is," Jessica whispered, which puzzled Nic because there was no one even close to them. "I swear it is."

Those last words sent Nic's gaze back to the three people at the statue as Jessica started walking that way. One was a little boy reading the plaques, a boy who looked painfully thin, as if he'd been sick or something. It was hard to be sure at this distance, Java Time was nearly two full blocks away from the statue, but she thought the woman was someone she'd seen in town occasionally, maybe somewhere else as well. She'd never seen her with a kid, though. And she had no idea why Jessica was so excited.

They crossed Ash Street and were nearly to Oak, now only a block from the statue, when her friend gasped, "It is him. It's really him. And that must be his little boy."

Finally, Nic shifted her gaze to the man beside the woman and little boy. He was looking at the child, not the statue, which she found interesting. Tall; she'd put him at at least a foot taller than her current student, the fifteen-and-a-half-hand palomino, so six foot plus. Nice build. Lean, but well muscled. He wore well-fitting black jeans, and a black canvas jacket that appeared to be lined in a blue-and-black plaid wool or flannel, a good choice on this chilly January morning.

She shifted her gaze to his face, now that he'd looked up from the little boy. He had a strong, masculine jaw, thick dark hair beneath a worn baseball cap with a logo she didn't recognize. A little stubble, but not too much. He was wearing sunglasses, which seemed a little odd on this mostly cloudy, chilly morning, but there could be reasons. She found herself wondering what color his eyes were behind the tinted lenses, which was a bit odd in itself; she didn't usually speculate about such things. It must be because Jessica seemed to recognize the guy, while she didn't. All she could be sure of was he wasn't a local, not because she didn't recognize him, but because everyone in Last Stand could just about quote by heart the story on that plaque he was now reading.

"He's even more gorgeous in person, isn't he?"

"I have no idea, because I don't know who you mean."

"It's Jackson Thorpe!"

The name rang a bell, but she didn't know why. So she asked the obvious. "Jackson Thorpe?"

Jessica stared at her as if she'd just asked who Sam Houston was. "Jackson Thorpe? Austin Holt?"

Now she was confused. "Don't know that name either. I

think I've heard or seen the Thorpe name, but—"

"Are you telling me you still don't watch *Stonewall*?"

It fell into place then. Even she, who spent most of her free time in the evenings reading or watching old favorite movies, had heard about the television series that it seemed everyone but her was rabidly watching. She'd tried it once, just to see what the shouting was about, and because it was set here in the Texas Hill Country, but when the opening credits swept over a few hills with towering, snowy mountains visible in the background, touting it as a place fifty miles southwest of Austin, she'd clicked it off in disgust. She had no patience for Hollywood's certainty that they could pass anyplace off for anyplace else. Places that really existed, anyway. She wouldn't have cared if they hadn't said where their fictional ranch was, but they had, and it ticked her off that it was so blatantly and obviously—to anyone who set foot out of their West Coast bubble—not just wrong, but insulting.

She knew hers wasn't the typical reaction, but she was Texas born and bred, as were her father and his father and his father before him, and she did not take kindly to either the lies or the myths someone who'd never lived here propagated about her beloved home state.

"You don't." Jessica was staring at her now. "The hottest thing on TV, and you don't even give it a shot?"

"A show filmed in California claiming to show Texas? Darn straight I don't."

"But it's the story that matters," said Jessica. She glanced toward the statue again. "Well, that and the gorgeous star." She sighed. "I suppose that's a girlfriend, although I don't remember—"

"She's from here," Nic interrupted before Jessica could start pouring out a flood of celebrity gossip that would only irritate her further.

Jessica frowned, looked almost disappointed. "She is?"

"I don't know her, but—" She broke off as it suddenly fell together in her memory bank. She had seen the woman around, but she'd also seen her picture in *The Defender*, the local paper, some years ago. A picture taken at the funeral of David Carhart, a Last Stand native who had been instrumental in updating and remodeling Creek Bend High School. She remembered he'd been young, barely thirty, and that it had been some fast-moving cancer.

"Wait, his sister moved here. I remember reading that!" Jessica said suddenly, her excitement rekindling. "So it must be her with him. That would make sense, that he'd visit her. They've both lost somebody," she said with a sigh that, had it been any deeper, would have been over-the-top dramatic.

"I know she lost her husband," Nic began.

Jessica nodded. "And he lost his wife, the little boy, his mother. So sad."

"Let me guess. Another Hollywood star he met on set and who left her husband for him, or some such Tinseltown drama?"

Okay, that was sour even for her, especially about a dead woman, and she didn't blame Jessica for giving her a shocked look. "Actually," her friend said, rather coolly, "she was a therapist. Kind of like you are for problem horses, only for children with special needs."

Now she really felt bad. "Sorry," she said with a grimace. "That was nasty and uncalled for."

As was her way, Jessica immediately forgave her. "You're just worried about your dad."

She couldn't deny that was true. Her father insisted he was fine after the mild—was there such a thing?—heart attack he'd had last summer, but she lived in constant fear of another, worse one.

And here you are mocking someone who's actually gone through what you feared, the loss of someone so close. Not to mention an innocent child.

"It does have me on edge. He's trying to do as much and work as hard as he did before. Especially since Clark retired. Even though we hired a couple of regular hands to pick up the slack." Their ranch manager had moved to Florida to be near his kids after working for the Baylors for over two decades.

"He just wants things back to normal," Jessica said. "You know your dad."

"Yeah, I do." She stifled a sigh. "He just won't ease up."

Jessica looked back toward the statue, where the three people still stood. The little boy reached out to touch the toe of Asa's boot, where many others had done the same, so many that the spot was a burnished gold rather than the dark bronze of the rest of the figure. But what caught her eye was the man's expression as he stared at the boy. He'd pulled off the sunglasses now, as if he hadn't been certain of what he was seeing. She saw then how tired he looked and felt even worse about her smart-ass comment.

Something about the way he was staring at the child— his son, if Jessica was right, and she probably was—grabbed at her. His expression seemed an odd combination of disbelief and hope. And in that moment she knew that, Hollywood or not, this man genuinely loved that boy.

"Can we go say hello?" Jessica asked hopefully.

"Hoping for a selfie?" Nic asked, but lightly, all her earlier snark vanished.

"Maybe," Jessica admitted with a grin.

Nic looked back at the trio. "He looks pretty serious right now. Do you want to intrude?"

"And now you're protecting him, the epitome of the Hollywood you hate?"

"I don't hate Hollywood. With a few exceptions, I mostly just ignore them. I was thinking more about the kid."

"Good point," Jessica said with a sigh. "Let's just head that way then, and what happens, happens."

"Or doesn't," Nic cautioned.

"That too," Jessica agreed.

At least her friend was less frenzied now, Nic thought, as

they started walking toward the library and the statue in front of it. Inwardly, she was shaking her head at Jessica's obvious infatuation with some Hollywood hunk who'd probably never even been close to a horse before he had to be.

But then she remembered that look on his face and decided anyone who loved his son that much couldn't be all bad.

Chapter Four

JACKSON TRIED TO tamp down the hope that had erupted almost painfully in his chest as Jeremy showed the first real interest he'd shown in . . . well, anything, since the day Leah's car had been launched off a bridge by a car that had just been jacked by a couple of L.A. thugs. Two people had died that night, including the owner of the stolen car, and Jackson had always felt bad for the family of the man whose name was barely mentioned because of the headline value of his wife's death. In the end, it only made him hate the media more than he already had, which was saying something.

Tris touched his arm, and he shifted his gaze to her, saw in his sister's eyes that she understood. Then she turned back to Jeremy.

"Would you like to see where it actually happened?" she asked the boy. "There are bullet holes and everything."

That got her a startled look, and again Jackson felt that hope. This was the most Jeremy had reacted to anything in nearly two years.

"It's right down there," she said, pointing up the street past what a sign said was the municipal courthouse. "Just across the street." She bent down to say in a whisper that was loud enough for him to hear, "It's in a saloon, and usually someone your age wouldn't be allowed in, but because it's history, they'll let you, as long as you don't ask for a beer."

Jeremy laughed. It was short, weak, but definite, and in that moment, Jackson could have kissed his sister. Would have, if he wasn't afraid it would derail the moment.

"Let's go," he said. "Real bullet holes from almost a couple hundred years ago? I wanna see this."

He held out a hand to Jeremy, and after a moment, the boy took it. Just the connection caused that hope to surge yet again, and he nearly shuddered under the impact. He didn't even mind when two women walking toward them on the sidewalk gaped at him. Well, one of them did, as she not so surreptitiously brought out her phone, probably for a photo. The other woman just looked at her companion, and somehow he knew she was rolling her eyes. Maybe it was her body language.

And that body speaks a language any man would understand . . .

He almost stopped in his tracks at the shock of that thought. Would have, if it hadn't been so important to keep moving with Jeremy. He hadn't gotten a message from that aspect of his life in . . . well, in two years. He'd thought that part of him had died along with Leah on that awful night. If it had never reawakened, he would not have been surprised. He'd adored Leah, and had never once strayed or even thought about it, despite the fact that he'd worked with women some considered the most attractive in the world.

They got closer, and he made himself look away before they made eye contact. But the image was so vivid in his mind, it was almost as if he were still staring at her. About a half a foot shorter than him, with long hair in a braid that reached halfway down her back. Hair that was the color of the sand on the beach that day that had, in essence, started all this. And blue-gray eyes almost the color of the ocean that had lapped at that sand. Dressed in snug, well-broken-in blue jeans and a matching denim jacket, he couldn't tell much more than she was slim and looked and moved as if she were quite fit.

Cowboy boots. She was wearing a pair of cowboy boots. Or would it be cowgirl boots? He didn't know. But they looked worn, also well broken in. Instinctively, he looked for the sign Tucker had told him to look for, the band of worn leather on the inside edge.

"If someone's really a rider," his best friend and stuntman had told him, "the stirrups will wear that part smooth and dark."

Since Tucker Culhane had been a rodeo cowboy here in Texas before he'd come west, Jackson figured he knew whereof he spoke. And on this woman, the signs were there.

At least he didn't get caught staring at anything but her feet.

Even as the thought went through his mind, he wondered about those feet, if they'd be sturdy and calloused, or slender and arched.

And just when did you develop a foot fetish?

He shook his head sharply and managed to give her companion a faint smile as she not-too-subtly snapped a picture with her phone. The woman looked as if she wanted to stop, to approach him, but the woman he had to work to keep from staring at stopped her with a touch on the arm and a couple of whispered words.

There had been a time when he would have paused, maybe chatted a little, and taken a selfie with her if she'd wanted it. But not now, he couldn't now, not when Jeremy was tugging at his hand as if he weren't moving fast enough. And in that moment, he shot the woman who had so caught his attention a look he hoped she would see as thankful.

For just an instant their gazes locked, and he stared into eyes that seemed as deep as that ocean he'd likened them to. He'd been lauded a lot for his own eyes, which had been called everything from dark blue to bottomless, but he found her lighter-blue eyes with that touch of gray much more appealing.

And the sooner he stopped thinking things like that about this total stranger who was likely to stay that way, the better.

Besides, he doubted he'd been mistaken about that flare of animus that had shown on her face in the moment before she looked away.

When they reached the white stone building on the next

corner, he saw there was another plaque commemorating the actual battle that had taken place here. He read the story of how a small group of locals had taken refuge in this, the only stone building around, when a swath of Santa Anna's troops had swept through during the Texas Revolution.

"Wow," he murmured, looking at the deep pits in the wall. "Look at that one, Jeremy. The bullet's still in there, from all those years ago."

The boy had to get up on tiptoe to see it, but he did. He reached into the hole, as if trying to reach the deeply buried chunk of metal, again showing more interest than he had in anything in far too long.

"This is where that guy"—Jeremy looked back the way they had come, toward the statue—"brought the bullets back to?"

"It is."

The voice came from the doorway, where a tall, dark-haired man with a short, neatly trimmed beard stood leaning against the doorjamb, his arms crossed over his chest as he smiled at Jeremy. He looked up at Jackson, and there was a flicker of recognition in his eyes. But he didn't say anything, and Jackson relaxed a little.

"You're Mr. Highwater, aren't you?" Tris asked.

"Slater, please. My brother's the Mister of the family."

Tris looked at Jackson. "He's the police chief, the one on the second plaque on the statue. And he's definitely a Mister. Or a Sir."

"Just Chief'll generally do," the man said.

Jackson's brow furrowed. "Your brother's the police chief and you . . ."

"Run the saloon. Yes." A grin flashed across the man's face. "It keeps life interesting." He looked back at Jeremy then. "You want the rest of the story?"

His son nodded, so quickly that hope was really starting to take root. The saloon owner continued his tale.

"They were outnumbered, five to one. But they knew from what happened at the Alamo that the Mexican troops had orders to kill, so they had no choice but to fight. They holed up here in the saloon, since the only other things here at the time were a stable and a trading post, both built of wood. The stone here held, but they ran out of ammunition and thought they were all dead. But that guy"—he echoed Jeremy's look at the statue—"saved them all with that ammo run."

"But he died," Jeremy said, his tone one of protest.

"He did, sadly," the man said. Jackson liked the way the guy was totally focused on the boy as he went on. "But the others lived, thanks to him. They fought until the troops gave up and moved on, and three months later Santa Anna was beaten soundly by Sam Houston at San Jacinto, in eighteen minutes."

"That's fast," Jeremy said, looking a little awed.

"Very fast. And so, because of Asa Fuhrmann's bravery, I'm here today to tell the story."

Jeremy gave the man a puzzled look then. "Huh?"

"One of those he saved was my great-times-five grandfather."

The boy's eyes widened. "He was here, back then?"

"He was. And the Highwaters have been here ever since. One took over the saloon, and his son became the county sheriff, and there's been a Highwater in each line of work ever since. I guess they decided since they'd nearly died for the place, they might as well stick around and make something of it. And so Last Stand was born."

Jeremy's expression turned to one of understanding. "That's why it's called that? Because there really was one?"

"Exactly," the man said with an approving grin. "Now, if you want to know the rest, all the details, you go into the library back there and find my wife, Joey. She'll get you the books that tell the whole story. There's even one my brother and sister-in-law did for kids, with some cool illustrations that really give you the feel of it. I think you might like it."

Jeremy looked up at Jackson. "Can we go there?"

"Absolutely," he said quickly. He glanced at Slater. "Just ask for your wife?"

"Or just look for her." A different expression crossed the saloonkeeper's face then, a warm, loving look Jackson recognized painfully well. "She'll be the very pregnant one."

"Congratulations," Tris said with a smile.

"Thanks." He winked at Jeremy. "And thanks for the practice. Haven't had much with kids and I'm trying to learn, so every bit helps."

A short while later they were in the library, and the definitely very pregnant librarian—the librarian and the saloonkeeper sounded like that rom-com he'd turned down a while back—lit up in that same way when they told her who had sent them. She quickly had Jeremy set up with a couple of books that he seemed to be intent on even more quickly.

"Thank you," Jackson said to her when she stepped back to stand beside them as Jeremy dug in. "I . . . my wife, his mother, died two years ago, and he's been totally withdrawn from the world ever since."

"That's horrible, for both of you. So this interest"—she gestured toward Jeremy—"is good?" It sounded more sincere than any of the platitudes he'd grown tired of.

"Very," Tris said, and proceeded to introduce herself. "I'm Trista Carhart. I live just down Hickory a ways, across from the park."

"Carhart? As in David Carhart, who spearheaded that wonderful updating of Creek Bend High?"

"Yes. I was his wife." Tris, being Tris, went on quickly to spare the librarian from having to come up with more condolences. "And this is my brother, Jackson, who's visiting. You might recognize his famous mug."

Jackson winced as she said it, but the librarian smiled and said only, "He does look familiar."

To his relief she left it at that, much as her husband had. She glanced over at the table where Jeremy sat. He appeared engrossed in the book with the colorful illustrations.

"Your husband mentioned that his brother and sister-in-law did that book?" Tris asked.

"Yes," Joey said with a smile. "There's a long story behind them, too, but that's theirs to tell. If you run into Kane or Lark, ask them."

This time Tris's brow furrowed. "Wait. Kane . . . Highwater?"

Joey nodded, and this time she let out a chuckle. "You've heard of him, I gather?"

"Is there anyone in the county—heck, in the state—who hasn't? So he not only has one of the greatest singing voices I've ever heard and writes beautiful music, he's an artist too?"

"That he is." She glanced at Jeremy again, then back to Jackson. "Do you think he might be interested in hearing the man who did the pictures for that book he's so engrossed in? Because if you'll still be here, he's playing here this summer, out at the Hickory Creek Inn, where he used to work."

"At this point, I'll try anything to keep this going," Jackson said, not caring if he sounded desperate. Because he was desperate. He'd had a glimpse today of the little boy he'd lost, the son he so loved.

And he'd do anything he had to, to bring that happy, curious, bright, laughing boy back.

Chapter Five

"COME ON, NIC, you've got to admit he's gorgeous."

"Kind of a requirement for his . . . work," Nic said.

It was an effort to maintain her usual dismissive tone, because Jessica was right. Jackson Thorpe was definitely a beautiful man. Not because of his looks, although they were exactly what appealed to her—great build, smooth moving, very male jaw line, and those eyes the color of a Texas sky just before the sun rose—but because of the expression in those eyes when he looked at his son.

While her overall opinion of actors stayed the same, she couldn't deny that this one had at least a bit of real life in him.

"Well, at least you agree he is," Jessica said, laughing as they paused in front of the office where she worked. They'd been friends since high school and got together whenever they could.

"I liked the way he was with his little boy," she admitted.

"That was sweet," her friend agreed. Then, with a rather pointed look, added, "But the way he looked at you was even sweeter. Holy cow, girl!"

"He was probably just wondering why I wasn't all goggle eyed over him, like you were."

She kept her tone teasing, but underneath, she was a bit . . . unsettled. As they'd walked back here, she'd nearly convinced herself she'd imagined that lingering gaze. And the way he'd practically yanked it away, as if he didn't want to get caught staring at her. Or didn't like that he had been.

But if Jessica had noticed it, too . . .

"I don't think he's like that," Jessica said. "Not every actor is, you know."

"I'm sure some aren't, but—"

"I read about how devastated he was after his wife was killed. It was heart wrenching. Would have been, even if I hadn't known who he was. He really loved her."

She bit back the first words that came to her, that he was an actor who could likely play that part to the hilt. She even reconsidered those words, because they didn't seem to fit the guy she'd just seen looking at his little boy with such love and heartache and yearning in those penetrating eyes. And if she had to admit he truly loved his son, why not his late wife too?

"I think," her friend said, in that tone that warned Nic she was about to get a Jessica assessment, statements that nearly always stung, but only because they were usually true, "you're just still soured on men in general, after Adam."

She went with her best defense. Best, because it was the

truth. "What I'm soured on are all the people who pretend, whether it's whoever decided to set that show in Texas, but film it in Caliphony-a, or the people who pretend to be cowboys, when the closest they've probably been to an actual cow is in the meat section of the market."

Jessica was grinning at her now. "Go ahead, say it. You haven't yet, but I know you're thinking it."

Nic grinned back as her best friend teased her back into good humor. "It's true."

"Yes. So say it."

And so she quoted her father's oft-stated wisdom. "The hat don't make you a cowboy."

They both laughed, hugged each other, and Jessica turned to open the door and go back to work. But then she paused and looked back.

"Next time you're online, go look at how Jackson Thorpe was, as they say, discovered. I think it might surprise you."

Nic thought about that all the way back home. Unlike many, she preferred to spend her time outside, with the horses she loved and trained, rather than cruising the internet, but she did indulge occasionally, and belonged to an online group of horse folks with a rather voluminous message board.

She paused at the gate to the ranch and got out to grab the mail from the mailbox. Her father still clung to his snail mail, and she didn't mind having paper copies, since half the stuff that came electronically, she had to print out, anyway, for various records.

The Baylor ranch was not what it had been in its heyday, but then what was? The Raffertys, maybe. Especially now that they'd combined with the Roth family who owned the neighboring ranch, through the unexpected marriage of the youngest Rafferty with the Roth daughter. The two had been mortal enemies most of their lives, yet now they were married and living in a newly built house that straddled the property line, signifying the melding of the two ranches and families.

But there was nothing like that in the cards for the Baylors. They'd had to sell off a third of their property to cover Mom's medical bills after her accident, and had only hung onto enough for Nic to keep her training business—which was thankfully flourishing—going, and for Dad to maintain his small purebred Black Angus herd. She told herself since Clark had been leaving, it was for the better. Not that she didn't still miss the man who'd been a big part of her life growing up, the gruff old soul who somehow hadn't minded when she showed up on the porch of his house on the far side of the largest pasture. And since they were only about two-thirds the size they used to be, they hadn't replaced him, and the house had stood empty. She loved the place, and had thought about moving in there herself, but couldn't quite bring herself to be so far from Dad this soon after his heart attack.

But it had all been worth it. Mom was still here, and if not quite the woman physically that she'd once been, she'd made up for it in other ways, adapting amazingly. And mentally she was still Mom, sharp as a tack and with that kindness of heart that was a bit of a miracle in itself, after all she'd been through.

She headed for the house to drop off the mail and see Mom, who turned out to be taking a nap. She knew Dad would be out checking on the cattle, aboard his beloved Spike. Her father was very particular, and his declaration that the big bay quarter horse was the best-trained he'd ever ridden was something she treasured and always would. Especially since the horse had come to them as a problem child she'd picked up at auction for much less than his bloodlines were worth. It had taken nearly eight months of work, six days a week, to get the recalcitrant bay to behave, and then learn the basics of his new life.

She'd even had to consult with local blacksmith Logan Fox when he'd come to replace a shoe her own Sassafras had tossed. The tall, lean, taciturn man was the closest she'd ever seen to a horse whisperer, and he and Spike had had a long conversation. Watching from outside the corral, she'd have sworn the animal was answering the man as he literally whispered to him. The snorting and head bobbing certainly seemed like answers, anyway. And she couldn't deny the animal was easier to deal with after three sessions with the man.

Fox himself was a mystery to her, and to most others in Last Stand. He lived a very quiet life in a cabin outside of town, was utterly reliable in his work, and was rarely seen outside of it. Even when he showed up at an area rodeo, it was because he'd been hired to be on standby.

The only other thing she knew about him was that he was an indefatigable reader. And she only knew that because she'd overheard him discussing some scholarly tome with Slater Highwater at the Last Stand Saloon the last time she and Jessica joined several other women for what they called the girls' night out, a monthly excursion to various voted-upon locations, but always ending back home in the saloon for a good-night drink. She'd meant to ask Joey Highwater if he was a regular at the library, but Joey had missed the next outing, having just found out she was pregnant, and after that joyous news, Nic had forgotten.

She picked her laptop up from the coffee table in the living room and carried it over to the kitchen counter. She turned it on and went for a bottle of water while it booted up. She needed to check the bank to be sure that last check had cleared, although this was for the third horse she'd trained for the Blakes, so she wasn't really worried.

The bank website confirmed her expectation, and she smiled with a little touch of the relief she always felt when she knew she had a few months' cushion in the account. In addition, she had two new horses coming in soon, which should buy them even more time. With Mom's tutoring jobs—once a teacher, always a teacher was her favorite saying—and as prolific as it appeared Dad's herd was going to be this spring, the outlook for the year was fairly solid. She was very thankful for that.

She was more thankful for the fact that she was able to contribute her part, doing what she loved most.

She decided to check the message boards before she shut down. She avoided the newbie group. She didn't have time at the moment to indulge in the long, involved answers most of them needed. There were a couple of positive comments on the barrel racing board about another answer she'd given, which she acknowledged. One of the moderators of the group had asked her about the Last Stand rodeo, saying he was considering coming down from Ft. Worth this year, and she gave him a quick recap of what he could and shouldn't expect.

She exited to the home page and was about to sign out when one of the groups she always ignored caught her eye— the group dedicated to discussing the representations of horses and their people in the entertainment media. And there was one topic with more posts than any other topic on the entire platform.

Stonewall.

She moved the pointer back to the sign-out icon. Hesitated. Reached again to click the button. Hesitated again.

With a muttered expression of disgust at herself, she went back and clicked the topic. Her screen exploded into what looked like dozens of different threads on every topic, from the storyline to the actors and, of course, to the horses.

I don't have time for this.

She moved to sign out again. This time something unexpected caught her eye. A post from some time ago titled simply "In Last Stand?"

That she couldn't resist and clicked. *Click bait. That's where the name comes from, and you just bit.*

It turned out only to be someone asking if it was really true Jackson Thorpe's sister—who apparently was a teacher, like Mom—lived in Last Stand. With several answers confirming it was. A couple of guys chimed in with opinions on her undeniable hotness, which the women countered with ratings of her brother on a scale of ten, with his final ranking a 9.8.

I couldn't argue with that. If I ever paid attention to such silly discussions.

Which, she admitted wryly, she just had.

With a grimace, she closed out the browser and shut down the laptop.

Chapter Six

JACKSON COULDN'T REMEMBER the last time he'd spent so much time in a library. But just sitting there, watching Jeremy read so intently, was worth every minute.

And personally, he was enjoying the fact that no one was bothering him. He doubted even a library back in L.A. would have protected him from the constant approaches of fans, anti-fans, and the giddy types with their ever-present cell phone cameras now called social influencers.

The boy had been obviously captured by the history of this small Texas town, and Joey the librarian had been wonderful about finding him books to read at his age level and, as she'd told Jackson, a bit above, since he was obviously capable of comprehending them. Jackson had felt a little burst of pride at that confirmation of what he'd always known—that his son was smart.

He sat there with the other book Joey had shown him, the first book done by her brother-in-law's wife who, she had mentioned, had worked for Child Protective Services before she'd had to leave because of the emotional cost of dealing with abused and damaged children. The picture book featured a comical, but clever, pony named Murphy, and was clearly aimed at very young children, but even as an adult, he could see the appeal.

"Why're you reading that little kid's book?"

Jackson looked up to see his son looking at him quizzically. He smiled. "Because Murphy's pretty funny."

"But it's for babies."

"Just because it's written for them doesn't mean it's no good for anyone else. Like your favorite comic, it's for you, but some grownups like it too."

"Oh." The boy seemed to accept the argument, because he shrugged and said, "I gotta go to the bathroom."

Since the facility was in his line of sight, Jackson just nodded and the boy scampered off. Even that made him smile. It had been so long since he'd seen the normal, high-energy kid his son had once been, every sign was balm to his battered soul. This was only their second day here, and he already knew it was the best decision he could have made.

He finished the whimsical story of Murphy the pinto pony, closed the book, and set it on the seat Jeremy had been using. He picked up the adult volume on Last Stand history Joey had given him, which he'd found as intriguing as Jeremy had found the youth version. He read a couple of pages, then looked toward the restroom, calculating how much time to give Jeremy before he went to check on him. Only the certainty that it would embarrass the boy mightily made him add an extra two minutes to his mental timer.

He read some more, then glanced toward the door to the restrooms again. This time Jeremy was there, just outside the door, talking—actually talking—to a woman standing there. Joey was with them, so he wasn't really concerned. Funny, how he already trusted her. Must be the librarian in her, he thought with an inward grin.

When he looked up again, the three of them were headed toward him, Jeremy in the lead, followed by Joey and the other woman, who—

Who was the woman from yesterday. By the statue.

He stood up slowly, oddly uncertain of his balance. Her hair was in the braid again, at the moment brought forward to trail down over the front of what looked like the same denim jacket she'd had on when he'd first seen her. The jeans were different, looked newer, but still well broken in. Under the jacket was a sweater the same sea blue as her eyes. And it fit . . . well. Clung in all the right places, and she had some very right places.

And he was reacting to them again. In that way he'd thought dead and buried with Leah.

"Dad, Dad, she's got horses. Can we go see them?"

Jeremy's excited voice yanked his attention back, perhaps the only thing that could have.

"What?" he asked, looking at the librarian, feeling like he had to shake off some fog.

"Jackson," Joey said, sounding a little self-conscious, despite the fact that he'd told her the "Mr. Thorpe" wasn't necessary. "This is Nicole Baylor. She is a horse trainer—*the* horse trainer in Last Stand—and she's invited Jeremy out to her family's ranch to see them, if it's all right with you."

"Please, Dad?" Jeremy asked. "She says they've got a pony too." A too-rare smile flashed across the boy's face. "My size. Like in the book you liked."

Bracing himself, he shifted his gaze to Ms. Baylor.

"Only if you're amenable," she said with a polite smile.

Oh, crap. She had one of those voices. Low, almost husky, the kind that had a man thinking all kinds of thoughts it was way, way too soon for. The kind that made you think of sleepy mornings after a passionate night.

He gave himself an inward shake. He had to focus on Jeremy now, and what was best for him. He was the reason they were even here, after all.

"That's very kind of you," he said noncommittally.

"I look at it as building the next gen of horse lovers," she said, the smile more real this time.

"Which keeps you in business?" He regretted it as soon as it was out, because it sounded rather like an accusation, and he hadn't meant it that way. "I didn't mean—"

He stopped when she waved a hand and said, "I don't deny that. But more importantly, I want to help assure they remain a big part of western culture. Because I happen to love them."

"So do I," he said simply, leaving it at that.

Something seemed to flicker in her gaze then, and he

wondered if she was deciding whether she believed him or not. He didn't blame her. He wasn't a guy who'd grown up around horses, although he'd always found them beautiful. But the personal connection had come to him later, the first time he'd gotten a crew job on a western film. He'd met Tucker then, and the onetime rodeo cowboy-turned stunt-man had introduced him to the reality of the creatures, and he'd fallen hard. He counted it as one of the three best and most life-changing days he'd ever had, the first two being when he'd met Leah, and when Jeremy had been born.

And Tucker Culhane had become his best friend.

"Joey says you're visiting Last Stand. Do you have a vehicle, or access to one? We're a few miles outside of town."

When he hesitated—and he hated that he had to, but this relatively newfound fame had its downsides, and not being able to trust people he didn't know was one of them— Jeremy moved. His too-thin shoulders slumped, and the unreachable child he'd been for so long started to reappear. He couldn't stand it. He looked back at Ms. Baylor.

"We're staying with my sister. We can borrow her car while she's at work, like we did today. If you're sure, I know Jeremy would love it." *And that's more important than anything else right now.*

"Then come," she said. She pulled out a phone, called up a map, and shared it to his when he was ready. "Tomorrow late morning would be good. I'll have some time to introduce Jeremy to our . . . shorter resident."

He couldn't help it . . . he smiled widely at that.

"We're going?" Jeremy asked him as she started to walk away. "Really?"

"We're going," Jackson confirmed. The withdrawn child retreated, and the light that had dawned in the boy's eyes since they'd come to Last Stand returned.

Ms. Baylor turned and looked back over her shoulder at them. "Do I need to apologize for yesterday?"

He blinked. Brow furrowed, he said, "Why? You . . . stopped someone from interrupting a kind of tricky moment."

Again, he saw something shift in her expression. As if she hadn't expected him to remember or maybe recognize her. As if any man breathing would forget a woman like her.

"I meant for being one of the few people in the country not to recognize you on sight. I don't watch much TV."

"Oh." He gave her a wry smile. "No apology necessary. My ego may have inflated, but it's not that huge."

As she continued on her way, he tried to figure out why her admission that she hadn't recognized him made him feel . . . good? That didn't make any sense, other than it was always a bit of a relief dealing with people who didn't. They were getting harder to find these days.

It wasn't until, after checking out a couple of books for Jeremy and one for him on Tris's library card, they were walking back out to Tris's compact SUV that it hit him. Maybe, just maybe, her admission that she hadn't recognized him yesterday, that she wasn't a fan, somehow made the way she'd been looking at him mean more. Made it more real, more genuine. Like she'd been simply a woman looking at a man she . . . what? Was trying to place? Figure out how he was connected to Tris, the local?

Or a man she was attracted to?

Get over yourself, Thorpe.

Tucker's oft repeated words, usually delivered with that laugh that reminded Jackson that the man had known him when he was nothing more than a wrangler or a background decoration on a set, ran through his head. And it gave him the strength to push the silly thoughts out of his head. He had no time for such things now, anyway.

He glanced at Jeremy and whispered a silent bit of thanks for that moment when the boy had wished aloud that a fictional place was real.

Chapter Seven

WHEN SHE'D MADE the impulsive invitation, Nic hadn't really thought about all the ramifications. She'd just seen that too-thin little boy with the sad history light up when Joey had told him about her and what she did.

Maybe his sister would come with them. Then she remembered he'd said they'd used her car while she was working, and Joey had mentioned she was a teacher. She'd almost forgotten that, because inwardly, she'd been surprised that he hadn't just rented some snazzy car while he was here. Or bought one outright. Another jab in the image she had of the Hollywood big shot.

The big chestnut she was working in the arena snorted and shook his head, as if he knew her mind was wandering. And he probably did; he was one of the most sensitive horses she'd ever worked with, and all it took was the slightest change in tension on the reins and he was alerted, waiting for a command. She made herself focus because this clever animal deserved her best. He was going to be an amazing show horse someday, had the potential to be the second coming of What A Wave, the horse that had won the world reining championship three years running. Wave's rider might have been Belgian, but that horse was an all-American Quarter Horse. Just like this one. And their workout today did nothing to change her mind.

She was just finishing up grooming him when her father rode in at the end of the barn. And just like that she was back face-to-face with a task she dreaded. She had to tell Dad, who didn't like *Stonewall* for the same reasons she didn't, that the star of the thing was going to be dropping in on them tomorrow. And she didn't know how to even bring it up.

Then her gut kicked out an answer. *Tell him the same way it happened to you.*

"How'd he do today?" Dad asked as he tied up Spike and began to unsaddle him.

"Great, as usual. He's going to be really something."

"Thanks to you."

She laughed. "I think he'd be amazing for anyone. He's just one of those great ones, Dad."

"That's my girl. Don't take the credit, even when you should."

She couldn't deny the obvious pride in his voice warmed her. But she couldn't let the wonderful feeling of it divert her.

"I met a little boy at the library this morning," she began.

"Always nice to know kids still read," he answered dryly, as he started to brush down Spike.

"This one does. But it was really sad. His mother was killed in a horrible car accident when he was only five, and apparently he's never been the same since."

Her father stopped his brushing and turned to look at her. "No wonder he got to you," he said quietly, and she knew he was thinking of how close they'd come to being in the same boat. She'd been twenty, and just the thought of maybe losing Mom had darn near wiped her out.

"Yes, he did. I've never seen eyes so sad." His father's had been sad, too, but that had been nearly overshadowed by worry. "Anyway, he kind of lit up a little when Joey Highwater told him about our place, and that I train horses. So . . ."

A warm smiled flashed across her father's face. "Let me guess. You invited him out here?"

She nodded. The smile was great, and she knew he meant it. At least he would until she told him the rest. "I did. How could I not, when it's apparently the first thing that's really interested him since his mother died, the idea of coming and meeting our horses? So he and . . . his father are coming tomorrow morning."

"Good. But what's the catch? I can see in your face there is one."

She let out a long breath and her mouth quirked at one corner. "His father is Jackson Thorpe."

Dad's brow furrowed. "Jackson—Wait, the actor? Stars in that show they try to pass off as set here in the Hill Country?"

"With the snow-covered mountains in the background of the intro, yeah."

Her father let out a disgusted snort. "Hollywood. Typical."

"Yeah."

She saw the moment when he got back to the matter at hand. "And he's coming here?"

"His little boy is, Dad. He's the reason. His father's just . . . required to get him here." She paused. "Actually, I was a little surprised he wanted to come along. Figured he'd send the kid off like it was summer camp. But he seems really, genuinely worried about him."

"Not acting?"

"Not about this." She said it with a certainty that surprised even herself. "I think he genuinely loves and is worried about his son. Besides, it's Jeremy who matters, not who his father is."

The smile he gave her then was such a potent combination of pride and love it made her throat tighten. "And that, my girl, you got from your mother."

She smiled back at him. "The highest of compliments. Speaking of Mom, I suppose I'd better go tell her."

Her father rolled his eyes. "Yes, do. I suspect you'll make her day."

"Why?"

"She won't admit it, but she likes the guy. Or the character he plays, at least." He frowned. "Speaking of which, why isn't he back in Hollywood, playing?"

She hadn't actually thought of that. "He must have taken time off. He can probably write his own ticket."

"While they what, shut down production?"

"They must have other stuff they can do while he's gone. He isn't in every single scene, is he?"

Her father's mouth quirked. "Ask your mother. She's been watching it on the sly."

Nic's brows rose. Then she smiled. "Well, I may have to suspend my distaste, then." She was all for anything her mother actually enjoyed, after the hell she'd been through.

When she went into the house, her mother was at her computer in the living room. When it had become obvious the wheelchair was going to be a permanent fixture, her father and Logan Fox, who apparently had many other hidden skills besides blacksmithing and horse whispering, had built a desk area for her in the corner of the living room, where she had more room to maneuver the chair. And as hard as it was not to constantly want to help, she and Dad had consulted the therapists and been told that unless she might be in danger of hurting herself, letting her handle as much as she could on her own was the best option.

It had worked, because now, besides the tutoring duties the former teacher still took on, Mom was the co-founder of a message board that connected thousands of wheelchair-using people around the world, to share stories, helpful hints, and hope. In her refusal to allow her accident to be the end of her productive life, Barbara Baylor was Nic's greatest inspiration.

She was clearly in the middle of something, typing up a post or a response, so Nic went and got herself a Dr Pepper out of the fridge. Mom looked over her shoulder at her, and she held up the can with a questioning look. She got a smile and a "Yes, please, honey," so she grabbed a second one.

By the time she got back across the room, Mom had finished the post and closed out the program. She spun the chair around to face her as she took the proffered can.

"Thank you," she said.

"You may be thanking me for more," Nic said with a warning grin.

Her mother's brows rose. "What? Why?"

Nic sat down so they'd be eye to eye. "I understand you've become a *Stonewall* fan on the sly."

Mom sighed. "Your father's been complaining?"

"Not really complaining, just . . . mentioning."

"Look, I know you don't like the show, and the way it's done, and I see your point."

"My only point is saying it's Texas doesn't make it so."

"I know that. But I enjoy it for the story, not the trappings. For the people."

"Including the star?"

She nearly laughed when she saw the faint tinge of pink rise in her mother's cheeks. "Well, even you can't deny he's an amazing-looking man. But that's not why I like him. Did you know that after his wife was killed, he went back to the hospital that tried to save her and spent a lot of time personally thanking the staff? And the other person who was killed that night, the man in the car that was stolen? He set up a trust fund for his two children and never said a word about it until the man's widow spoke up, months later."

Nic was staring at her mother now, a little stunned.

"And then he came back to the hospital several times, going around and talking to patients, and their families, whoever was there. Brought attention to the needs of the hospital, which brought in donations. Along with what he gave them himself."

She stared at her mother. "I . . . no, I didn't know any of that."

"One of the people in my online group met him that way while she was in the same hospital. He told her it was the only thing that helped, seeing people still fighting. And he came back several times to the children's ward. With his little boy, hoping it would help him too."

This was yet another puncture in her balloon of dislike, and it took her a moment to make herself focus on the reason she'd come in to see her mother. "Well, in that case, I have a surprise for you. He's coming here."

"To Texas?" Mom asked. "I'm not surprised he's coming again."

That interrupted Nic's train of thought once more. "Again?"

"Well, yes, he's been here a few times, I've read, to get the feel, he said. And his best friend, his stuntman, is from Fort Worth. He says he relies on him a lot."

She was shaking her head with amusement now. "Any more star gossip you'd like to spill before I clarify what I meant?"

"Clarify?"

"He's coming *here*, Mom. To the ranch."

Her mother stared at her. "What?"

She drew in a breath and told the whole story again. And she saw the moment when her mother's reaction changed from one of shock to one of sweet concern. "Oh, that poor child. That was a good thing you did, Nicky. I know you don't like the man."

Instead of repeating that it wasn't the man, it was the misrepresenting of this state she so loved that she didn't like, she repeated what she'd said to her father. "It's Jeremy who matters, not who his father is."

"And that's the daughter I love," her mother said with a warm smile.

And as she leaned over to hug her mother, all she could think of was the little boy who no longer could.

Chapter Eight

JACKSON KNEW THAT some people disliking him without even knowing him came with the territory. And it happened often enough that he'd grown able to recognize the signs. He'd known from the moment Ms. Baylor had looked away from him there on the main street of Last Stand that she was one of them. Whether it was his success—it had come so fast a lot of people thought he didn't deserve it—or his profession in general, he didn't know. And frankly, didn't care. All he cared about was the look of gentle, kind compassion that had come into those ocean-colored eyes when she looked at Jeremy.

And the fact that now his son was peering out the car window with every evidence of excitement. You'd think they were on their way to a major amusement park or something. Back when such things had been able to excite the boy.

He slowed down, glancing at the map on Tris's car's display. They should be there, or very close, but he didn't see a house or anything that—

"Dad! Is that her?"

He looked in the direction Jeremy was pointing. Saw a

horse and rider. The horse was a reddish brown with a light-colored mane and tail, almost the shade of the hair of his rider. Because yes, there was no doubt in his mind that was Nicole Baylor. She sat a horse with the same ease as Tucker. The ease that came from riding since childhood. He himself was a pretty decent rider, thanks to Tuck, although he always felt like he needed to get better. But he flat-out loved horses and hoped that made up a bit for what he might lack.

And this horse was almost as gorgeous as his rider, with that flaxen mane and tail flying as he moved in a steady, ground-eating lope. Ms. Baylor—he'd found it best to think of her that way, to rein in his unexpected response to her—barely moved in the saddle, and he had the feeling that if something spooked the horse and he went crazy sideways, she'd stay put as if part of the animal. But then, from what Joey at the library had said, he kind of doubted any horse she'd trained would go haywire unless it was something serious.

Like a rattlesnake or some other charming resident . . .

"She rides really good, like you and Uncle Tucker, doesn't she?" Jeremy said as she waved them to the north.

"Probably better than me, at least," he muttered as he turned his attention back to the thankfully empty roadway.

He saw what looked like a gate up ahead and thought he must be right when she headed that way. When they got there, he saw it was definitely a turnout to a gate, marked with two simple signs, BAYLOR BLACK ANGUS and NICOLE

BAYLOR HORSE TRAINING. Nothing fancy, but then perhaps they were so well-known for each vocation, they didn't need fancy signs. Tris had said Nicole certainly was. Even she, who didn't dwell in horse circles, had heard her name.

She reached the gate just as he was slowing Tris's car to a halt. She dismounted and in one smooth, continuous movement, pulled the reins over the horse's head to drop on the ground.

"Why did she do that?" Jeremy asked.

"It's called ground-tying," Jackson answered, although he never took his eyes off the woman who was now unlocking the gate. "They train the horse not to move when the reins are on the ground like that. So they don't have to tie them to anything."

"Wow," Jeremy said.

"Yeah," Jackson said. Then, as it suddenly occurred to him, he got out of the car and went to help with the big gate. He'd been so busy watching the graceful way she moved he'd completely forgotten everything else. But as it turned out, she didn't need any help. The apparently counterbalanced structure swung open easily.

"Slick," he said.

She smiled. "My dad's a bit of a genius with stuff like that."

Funny, he thought. She seemed more . . . something today. Maybe she'd just resigned herself to the fact that doing this incredibly kind thing for Jeremy meant putting up with his father too. Because that negative look she'd given him in town was nowhere to be seen—or felt—today.

"Head on up," she called out to him. "Just veer right at the split and that'll take you to the barns."

He nodded, then said, "Thanks again for doing this. He"—he tilted his head back toward the car and Jeremy—"is happier about this than he's been about anything since his mother was killed."

"I'm glad," she said, and there was no doubt in his mind that she meant it.

She walked back to the horse, and she was aboard before he even turned around to go back to the car. He wasn't sure her left foot had even touched the stirrup. He had a sudden vision of her doing one of Tucker's stunts, one he had gladly turned over to his friend, where he mounted a horse already at a dead run. He had little doubt she could pull it off, and probably had.

And he focused on that, so he didn't spend time thinking about how good she looked in those jeans, or how much he'd like to see her hair out of that braid that ran halfway down her back.

The farther they went up the drive, the more excited Jeremy got. "Do you see Nic?" he asked, looking in all directions.

He glanced at the boy. "Nic?"

"She told me to call her that," Jeremy explained. "Back at the library."

"Oh." It was all he could do not to laugh out loud at himself for even wondering why Jeremy was allowed that while he was still in the "Ms. Baylor" zone.

Because she doesn't like you or what you do. Best remember that.

Under other circumstances, with other people, he might try to charm her. He'd learned a lot in his world about how to do that, and even pulled it off now and then. It was easier there, though, where he had some standing. Where—as his thankfully out-of-the-country-at-the-moment agent kept telling him—he was the hottest property in town.

All of which meant nothing to this woman whose life was utterly based in reality. He wondered if there was anything produced in his industry that she did like. Old west westerns, as opposed to those set present day, like *Stonewall?* Or maybe she went for thrillers, or science fiction, or history-based things. He couldn't quite see her being enamored of rom-coms, but he didn't know her well enough to be sure.

Face it, Thorpe, you don't really know her at all.

And it didn't matter that he didn't. It didn't matter that she didn't care for his work, or he himself. All that mattered was that she was kind enough to worry about a little boy she'd just met enough to invite him to her home to meet her horses.

He pulled the car over next to a black pickup truck that had a logo painted on the door for Baylor Black Angus, figuring that was a safe enough place to park. He'd barely stopped before Jeremy was opening the car door.

"Be careful," he said as the boy scrambled out. "We don't know if the animals are used to having kids around."

Jeremy muttered something he was probably better off not hearing. He got out of the driver's seat and found Ms. Baylor, already dismounted, watching him. He couldn't interpret her expression, except that it held a touch of surprise. Did she think he was that ignorant of horses and cattle that he didn't realize a small, quick, unknown creature they weren't used to could startle them? Or did she just think he was an overprotective father, a helicopter parent, or whatever they called them these days?

He almost laughed at himself again, then. He sounded so old, even in his head. But he'd aged a hell of a lot in the last two years, and not by choice.

"Something funny?" she asked.

"Just me, feeling like I'm a hundred and ten."

For some reason that made her smile. But then she turned to Jeremy and proceeded to formally introduce him to the horse she'd been riding, her own personal mount.

"This is Sassafras, which is what they originally called what's now root beer. I just call him Sass, because he's full of it."

Jeremy grinned. And once more Jackson felt his eyes begin to sting and he had to look away. For this, just for this simple thing, a grin from his little boy, he didn't care if she hated him down to the bone.

When he lifted his gaze, she was watching him again, and this time there was a touch of that warmth he'd seen yesterday in her eyes.

"Come on," she said, turning back to Jeremy. "Let's head to the barn, and I'll introduce you to Pie. He's just about your size."

As they walked toward the big wooden building, Jackson noticed a narrow, paved pathway that led from the barn to what he guessed was the ranch house, a rather sprawling, metal-roofed single story that looked as if it had a couple of wings that had been added on. It was tidy, clean, and well kept. There was a big porch that ran the width of the building, with expansive steps leading down to a raised garden bed he imagined was quite something in the spring. And at the far end of the porch was a ramp of some kind.

"It's for my mother."

His gaze snapped back to the woman walking almost beside him; Jeremy was dancing—there was no other word for the excited quick step he was doing—ahead of them.

"The ramp, and the path," she said. "It's for my mother. She's in a wheelchair, but she likes to keep an eye on things, so my dad did it for her so she could get around."

He didn't know what to say about her mother, so he stuck with the other option. "Your dad must be really handy."

"He's the best," she said simply. "But by way of warning, my mother will probably show at some point if you bring

Jeremy back." Her mouth quirked. How had he not noticed how luscious it was before? "She's not here today, but she is a *Stonewall* fan, as I've just learned yesterday."

"You just learned?"

She shrugged and looked away from him, as if embarrassed. "She never told me because she knows how I feel."

So he'd been right. He hadn't imagined the negative vibe he'd picked up that first day in front of Asa Fuhrmann's statue. She didn't like him. Maybe even disliked him. Or the character he played. These days he didn't know which, not that it mattered much. To a lot of people, the two were inseparable. Even more so since this was the first major role he'd ever had, so there was nothing to balance it out, nothing for people to say, "I hate him in this, but he was good in that," about.

The realization made his own reaction to her even more unsettling. Then again, maybe it was better this way. He had no business thinking about things like how much he liked those eyes, or the way she moved, any of that. Not when Jeremy was so deeply mired in his grief Jackson was afraid the bright, loving child he'd been might never surface again.

And she was helping with that. No matter how she felt about him, she'd immediately picked up on Jeremy's distress and moved to help. That told him all he needed to know about her. And that's what he needed to focus on, not his totally unexpected attraction to her.

He had no time for—or right to—that.

Chapter Nine

"**I**'VE NEVER SEEN him take to someone like this." Nic watched the boy and the black-and-white pinto pony, a little amazed. "He usually has to be bribed with an apple or carrot."

"Aw, you're just sayin' that," Jeremy said, but he looked pleased, anyway, as he stroked the little pony's neck.

"If I were you," said his father, who was leaning against the corral fence, "I'd believe her. I don't think she says things just to say them."

And that pleased her in turn. Enough that she had to look away. She did not want to like the guy, but he was making it difficult not to. Especially when the way he looked at the boy made it so darned obvious he adored his son.

Her mother's words from last night floated up out of her memory.

He left, Nicky. He just walked away. All of Hollywood is abuzz over this. Nobody can believe somebody would walk away from something as huge as Stonewall *is right now. The show people are in an uproar, not knowing what to do because they don't know if he'll be back.*

Her mother had looked both shocked and disappointed

when she'd cornered Nic as she cleaned up after dinner last night, Mom's luscious chicken marsala. She'd obviously been doing some internet searching.

"But he did it for a good reason," she'd said.

How on earth had she ended up defending the guy she didn't even like? Because it was true, she answered herself silently. It had been for a good reason. And she had to admit, walking away from the kind of money he was likely getting paid was a sign of true dedication.

"They're leaving it open, I hear," Mom had gone on. "Not killing off the character. He's going to go missing or something."

"So they're going with reality?" She'd asked it a little too sweetly, and her mother had given her that look that told her she'd gone a bit too far. "Sorry, Mom. I know you like the guy."

"And, you should perhaps remember, I have excellent taste in men."

She'd glanced toward the man coming into the kitchen with the last of the dinner dishes. And Nic could do nothing else but agree. Because her father was the prototype for Nic's ideal man. So far in her life, she'd never met his match.

And that still held, because this man who pretended to be someone else for a living wasn't even close.

She suppressed a little shiver now as she remembered how she'd nearly dropped the plate she'd been putting in the dishwasher at the shock of even thinking about Jackson

Thorpe in that way. As big as he'd gotten, as fast as it had happened, had to have made him think he could do no wrong. She'd dealt with an ego like that once and was not about to try again. And there she went again, thinking about it as if it were even a possibility. On either side.

My ego may have inflated, but it's not that huge.

His words came back to her now, as she watched him smile at his son as he stroked Pie's dark nose. Maybe his ego wasn't huge by Hollywood standards, but it would probably overshadow anybody she knew. Currently, anyway, and as long as she stayed out of Austin.

"If you want to brush him, he'll be your friend for life," she said to Jeremy, who lit up at the idea. She got him the brush, instructed him to follow the way the hair grew, and he got to it.

"Why is his name Pie? Does he like to eat it?"

She smiled at the boy. "No, although he probably would if he got the chance. Pie is short for piebald, which is what they call a black-and-white pinto, as opposed to a brown-and-white one."

"Oh." The boy's serious expression gave her the distinct feeling he was filing that away as important knowledge.

For several minutes they just watched the pair, Nic with amusement, his father with an expression resembling . . . joy? That thought rattled her a bit for some reason she didn't want to analyze right now.

Very quietly, so quietly Jeremy wouldn't hear, he spoke.

"I know I've said thank you before—"

"And you don't need to again," Nic cut him off, but nicely. "Seeing any child this happy is a good thing, but one with his backstory? It's wonderful."

"That's very . . . understanding of you."

"I was nearly in the same boat. And the thought of losing my mother nearly broke me, even at the age of twenty. I can't imagine how horrible it must have been for him, so young."

"We wouldn't have made it if not for Tris."

"Your sister?" She remembered the woman who'd been with him that first day by Asa's statue, the woman with dark-auburn hair, but those same deep-blue eyes.

He nodded. "She essentially moved in with us right after it happened and stayed for nearly a year. I tried to convince her to stay permanently, but she missed this place." His mouth twisted into a wry grimace that was very expressive, and she couldn't help wondering if he used that to effect while playing his part. "And she doesn't much care for L.A."

"I'm with her on that one," Nic said dryly.

"I got that impression," he said, a shade too neutrally. Obviously she hadn't hidden her distaste very well.

"Last Stand is a great place," she said. "I wouldn't live anywhere else."

"You were born here?"

"Right here in Jameson Hospital," she confirmed. "My family has been here a long time. Not as long as the originals, but we love it just as much."

"The originals?"

"That's what I call the families who have been here since the last stand. The Raffertys, the Valencias, the Highwaters."

"Highwater. That's the guy who runs the saloon, who's married to the librarian."

She nodded. "And his oldest brother's our police chief, and a fine one. The other brother's a detective. Their sister runs their ranch, which is one of the bigger ones in the area."

"As big as yours?"

She had to tell herself he didn't know, couldn't know, how that stung, but it hurt, nevertheless. "Bigger, now. Much bigger."

It came out stiffly, sourly, but she couldn't help it. It was a very sore spot with her and probably always would be.

Jeremy ran over and looked up at her. "Nic, do you think . . . is he . . . could I ride him sometime?"

She'd expected that would come, eventually. Fortunately, the little pinto was good-tempered and amenable enough to even ignorant riders, which was why she'd chosen him for Jeremy to meet first.

"Well," she said, drawling it out, "let's see here now. You're both about twelve hands high, so that's a good fit."

The boy's brow furrowed. "Hands?"

"Yep." That was all she said. And she admitted she wanted to see if his father would—could—answer him. He did.

"That's how they measure how big horses are," Thorpe

said after a moment of silence, giving her a sideways look, as if he'd guessed what she was doing. What *was* she doing? Testing him? Why the heck would it matter? "They're measured at the withers, which is like their shoulders."

Jeremy turned his head to look, and at the right spot, she noticed. "But what's a hand? I mean I know what a foot is, for measuring, but . . .?"

"Same principle," his father said. "But back in the old days, they didn't have measuring tapes handy. So what do you suppose they measured with?"

It only took a matter of seconds for Jeremy's eyes to light up. "Their hands!"

"Yep," he said, and she wondered if he was echoing her on purpose. "It wasn't exact, because people's hands are different sizes, but it was at least a way to get a good idea."

"And nowadays a hand is generally considered four inches," Nic put in, trying to suppress her approval for how he'd done that, made the boy think it through and get to the answer himself. She didn't want to like anything about this guy, and it bugged her that she did. "So was I right? Are you about four feet tall?"

Jeremy nodded. "Someday, maybe, I'll catch up to my dad."

"I don't know. He's pretty tall."

She glanced at the man just a couple of feet away. Even as she looked, he was turning away. He took a couple of steps to his right and stopped. She watched, puzzled, until she saw him take a swipe at his eyes. And realized he'd stepped away to be out of his son's line of sight. So the boy wouldn't see him cry? And why was he, anyway?

She wasn't sure what made her do it, but after a quick look to see that Jeremy was engrossed again in his task of brushing Pie, she followed him. "He's enjoying this," she said.

He didn't look at her, but he answered. "Yes. He is."

"And that upsets you?"

He did turn then. "If by upset you mean I feel like my heart's going to explode, then yes. He used to say things like that all the time, but not once since . . ." His voice trailed off, and he looked away again. She gathered that simple exchange about Jeremy someday being as tall as his father had really struck home. She saw him swallow, hard, and his voice was beyond rough when he finished it. "Leah used to tell him all the time he would be as tall as me someday. It's so linked to her, it's . . ."

"Painful?" she asked.

He nodded, still not looking at her. She chose her next words carefully, because this was for the boy's sake. All of this was for his sake.

"Don't you think it's painful for him too?"

His head snapped around. "That's what I meant. Do you think I can even register how much anything about her hurts me, when I see him in such pain?"

It took some effort on her part not to cringe away from

his anger. And more effort to say, quietly, "I only meant that it might be a good thing, for him, if he sees that he's not alone in his pain. That you're hurting right along with him."

"Oh, he knows that," the man said bitterly. "I'm the father who went off the edge and on a month-long bender after she died. If Tris hadn't snapped me out of it, I don't know what would have happened."

She wondered how his sister had managed that, if it had taken some kind of sibling connection she didn't have, or understand, to do it. But she didn't ask, said only, "Good for her, then."

"She's been there. She gets it. And she saved us both."

"Using her own remembered pain," Nic said, marveling a little at the strength that must have taken. She had the feeling Trista Thorpe Carhart was someone she'd like to know.

"Yes. Compounded, because she loved Leah too. Hell, everyone did."

His late wife must have been a heck of a woman. She found herself wondering more about her, but didn't want to ask. She didn't stop to analyze why, just dropped it.

"Let's get that fledgling cowboy geared up for a ride," she said.

And as she headed for the tack room for the pony's gear, she tried not to wonder why she'd wanted to know more about a woman who'd died two years ago.

Chapter Ten

WHY ON EARTH had he vomited all that out?

Jackson tried to focus on the GPS map, but he didn't really need it now that they were on the edge of Last Stand. The town's layout wasn't all that tricky, mostly a square grid once you were inside the limits.

"Dad?"

He glanced over at Jeremy, and memory rushed over him, nearly swamping him. It had taken weeks after Leah's death to get the boy into a vehicle without screaming protests. He understood it. He was a bit paranoid about it himself. In those early days he'd almost taken Miles's offer to have someone pick him up and get him to wherever they were shooting that day, but that idea was at war with the thought of surrendering what little control he had left in his life. Nor would he let anyone else drive the protesting Jeremy, not just because of the boy's distraught state, but because he didn't trust anyone else to be as hyperalert as he would be with his son in the car.

"What?" he asked, pulling himself out of the memories with what was still an effort, even after two years.

"Can we come back tomorrow?"

"Ms. Baylor said you could."

"Yeah, but I didn't know if you would. And why do you call her Ms. Baylor?"

He gave Jeremy a sideways look and a rather lopsided smile. "Because, unlike you, she hasn't given me permission to call her anything else."

"Oh." The boy's brow furrowed. "Why?"

"You'll have to ask her, but I suspect she doesn't like actors much."

"Is that why she doesn't watch *Stonewall*?"

"Again, you'll have to ask her."

Although those last questions hadn't been comfortable, it was better than stewing about why he'd poured half his guts out in front of this woman who didn't even like him. It had to have been in reaction to seeing Jeremy actually having fun for the first time in two years. He would have done much more than spill a chunk of his sad story for that.

"I will," Jeremy said solemnly.

He almost wished he hadn't said it, because he could imagine the way that would go.

Nic, why don't you watch my dad's show?

Because he's a fake cowboy, Jeremy.

And the weirdest part was, he couldn't blame her for that. She lived the life. She was the real deal, and no doubt knew many actual, genuine cowboys. Why would she care about Hollywood's idea of them?

"So . . . we can go back tomorrow?"

"Why don't you ask your aunt if she'd like to go? Since it's Saturday." And maybe I can avoid it altogether. Something about being with someone who so clearly didn't like him or what he did for a living was surprisingly draining.

Although he had to say she was wonderful with Jeremy. Understanding, kind, welcoming . . . just not with him. But then, he didn't need it. Jeremy did. And that was all that mattered.

As it turned out, Tris said she'd love to go. "I've heard about Nicole often, usually after the rodeo, when she's trained half the horses who compete. And I've seen her around town occasionally, but I've never really met her."

"Rodeo?" Jeremy asked, that reborn curiosity of his showing in his face. "A real one, like Uncle T did, with bucking horses and roping cows and stuff?"

"Exactly. Last Stand has one of the biggest in the area, every July."

"July? Oh." Jeremy looked suddenly crestfallen. Jackson caught his sideways look before the boy said in a tone that matched that look, "We'll be back home so I can't go."

"Things can change," Tris said gently. "You never know."

It was later, after Jeremy had gone to bed, that she asked, "I gather you would rather not go with us tomorrow?"

"It's more, she would rather I didn't."

Tris lifted a brow. "You really believe that?"

"That she doesn't like me? Yeah, I do."

"Or is it your profession she doesn't like?"

"Right now, that's all it takes," he said, his tone a bit sour.

"Hmm. It's not like you showed up in boots and a cowboy hat."

He let out a short, sharp laugh at that. "As if I'd dare, here in real cowboy country."

"But that's the point. You *know* that would be a mistake. Unlike some, who do just that and then wonder why Texans roll their eyes."

Jackson studied his sister for a long, silent moment before saying, "You truly are a Texan now, aren't you?"

"David was, and he taught me. I like to think I learned well."

"You did." He hesitated, then added, "And he was a good teacher."

"The best," she said. "I work hard to be half as good as he was in my classroom."

"I don't need to see you in your classroom to know that you are. I just watch you with Jeremy." He sighed deeply. "I'm sorry I wasn't there for you the way I should have been when he died. The way you were for me."

"You had a newborn to worry about. And after Leah's rough delivery, she needed a lot of help. I understood."

"But once she'd recovered, I should have—"

She held up a hand to stop him. "By then you had another newborn to deal with, a newborn TV show. The chance of a lifetime, bro. A career-maker."

The smile she gave him was one hundred percent pure love and understanding. It struck him then, the connection he hadn't yet made. His loving sister's gentle kindness with Jeremy, and he himself, from the day Leah had been killed until now, had been a revelation to him. And the way Nicole Baylor had been with Jeremy took it a step further, the concept that when people are hurting, you help, even if they aren't your family.

And for Jeremy's sake, he would let her help, no matter what she thought of him.

NIC FOCUSED HER attention on the boy on the pony, not just because this was only his second time riding the little pinto, but because it helped her ignore the fact that she'd been almost sorry when Jeremy had turned up with only his aunt today.

She'd been walking Pie on a lead around the perimeter of the corral for about fifteen minutes now, and both pony and rider were doing well. He quickly got the idea of reining gently, coordinating hands and heels, and moving with the animal.

"You ride like you've ridden before," she said to him.

"I have. Dad let me, and Uncle T helped teach me."

"Uncle T?"

"His name's really Tucker, and he's not really my uncle, not like Aunt Tris is my aunt, but he's Dad's best friend. And his stuntman."

That startled her, that someone of Jackson's stature in the business would have a mere stuntman as his best friend.

"So he's the one that makes your dad look so good on horseback?" She made sure her tone was light and teasing, since she didn't want the boy to take offense on his father's behalf.

The boy half shrugged in the same manner she'd seen that father do. "Dad can do most of it, but then Uncle T wouldn't have a job. So he tells them he can't."

She blinked. Jackson Thorpe could do his own stunts, but didn't, so his best friend would have work?

"And where did your dad learn to ride so well?"

"Uncle T, mostly. He used to be a rodeo guy."

The combination of the name and this bit of info tripped something in her memory. "What's your uncle T's last name?"

"Culhane."

She stopped dead. Pie stopped immediately beside her. Jeremy looked surprised, but didn't wobble in the saddle. "Your father's best friend, your surrogate uncle, is Tucker Culhane?"

Jeremy gave her a rather puzzled look. "Don't know what sur-gate means, but yeah."

Tucker Culhane had been the biggest thing in rodeo for four years running, until he'd been pinned against a fence by a literal raging bull. He'd been hurt badly enough to retire from the circuit, although she'd seen he'd gotten back on his feet fairly soon, through what the article she'd read said was pure, stubborn Texas determination.

That had been, if her memory served, about a year before *Stonewall* had hit the air and almost instantaneously taken off. So he'd gone from riding bulls to doing stunts for Hollywood? She'd missed that part of his story.

After another half hour spent trying the boy aboard Pie at a trot, the most difficult gait to ride, she let him urge the pony into a slow, easy lope. By the time they'd made the first circuit of the corral, Jeremy whooped happily. Any instruction she gave, the boy followed, and Pie was always calm, so she felt confident in letting them off the lead. And when she finally did—with stern instructions about just how fast he could go—he whooped again.

She walked back to the fence, where his aunt was sitting on the top rail, watching.

"I cannot thank you enough," the other woman said. "I was afraid we'd never see him happy again."

"You're more than welcome. It does me good to see him like this, too, even though I've only just met him."

"You're so good with him. Like you've done this before."

"Not me. If you want to see the one who's really good at this, you should see my mother. She's done some riding therapy with kids. Nothing like a kid mired in grief seeing a woman who can't walk, get in the saddle and go."

Tris gave her a surprised look. "I'm sorry. I didn't realize."

"No reason you should. She's been a wheelchair user for a decade now, since a car accident damaged her spine."

"But she still rides?"

"She does," Nic said, always happy to express her pride in her mother. "Dad made some adaptations to her favorite saddle, a seat belt of sorts, and what she calls, with a laugh, tie-downs for her legs, since otherwise, they'd just flop around loose. And we worked with her horse until he understood all commands would be coming from hands, weight shifts, and voice from now on."

"By we, do you mean you?" Tris said with a smile.

Nic smiled back, but refused to take all the credit. "It took both of us, because that horse adores her. And Dad did his part." She nodded toward the side of the barn, where there was a setup of a long ramp with an easy slant up to a platform, and beside it a set of freestanding steps. With just enough room between for a horse to stand. "The steps were already there, for when I was too short to climb aboard, but the ramp is for her. Hand built."

"He constructed that whole thing?"

Nic nodded.

"You know," Tris said, with an approving nod in turn, "that's what I love about Texans. See a problem, come up with a solution."

Nic smiled widely. She liked this woman. Truly liked her. Enough to say teasingly, "It's a good thing she wasn't home when your brother was here yesterday. She probably would have been all over him like some rabid fan."

"He's very good with fans," Tris said. "Believe me, he understands they're why he is where he is." She paused, frowned. "Or rather, was where he was."

Her words reminded Nic of the article she'd read last night, when she was trying to get to sleep after an . . . interesting day. It seemed to her a weird quirk of the world, or of human nature, that suddenly, she kept seeing stories about him. She knew they had to have been there before, but he wasn't on her radar before, so she hadn't even noticed them. But now that his name had slammed into her brain, it seemed like they were everywhere.

The article had been speculating on the rumors running rampant. She remembered the lead line on the article vividly.

Rarely in Hollywood has anyone hit it as big and then vanished as fast as Jackson Thorpe.

She had almost stopped there, and before two days ago, before she'd met him in person, she would have. But now she didn't seem to have the self-discipline to ignore the rest of the online piece.

Thorpe's modern-day western television series set on a fictional ranch in Texas—but filmed mostly else-

MAKING A TEXAS COWBOY

where, she had muttered aloud while reading—*is the hottest thing going, so hot he could write his own ticket. Once he was riding high, both at work and at home, where he has often said his wife and young son kept him balanced.*

But now, after Leah Thorpe's tragic death, friends and workers on Stonewall *say he has never been the same. Is that the reason he seems to have disappeared? There had been rumors of heavy drinking, but they seem to have faded away, just as Thorpe now has.*

Production has been halted, although the official word is that this is only temporary. My not-so-official sources say the writing room is scrambling, with one rumor being they've been tasked to write Thorpe out of the show. So will the season currently being shot end in tragedy for Austin Holt? Check back here, and you'll know as soon as we do!

She remembered scowling as she closed out the article, wondering how she'd gotten sucked into what was so obviously a trashy gossip site. She might not like the guy, but he'd been through a painful kind of hell and didn't deserve to be treated like this. As if all that mattered was the damn show, and not the fact that his wife was dead and his child motherless.

The child he so obviously loved.

Chapter Eleven

H E WAS HOPING word hadn't gotten around that he was here, or that the residents here felt like Ms. Baylor did, that he should be ignored if not downright avoided. But since the only mode of transport he had at the moment was his feet, he was going to have to risk it, or stay holed up in Tris's half of this duplex the entire day.

He should have just rented a car at the airport, but at the time he'd been obsessed about getting Jeremy here, and when Tris said she'd pick them up, he hadn't thought beyond that. He wondered if there was someplace in town that rented vehicles. Maybe the place was too small. It was tiny, compared to the simultaneously sprawling and piled-high city he'd been living in. Even the suburbs had a crowded sort of feel to them, as if they were feeling the pressure of the huge metropolis just over the hill.

But here, even though he was only a couple of blocks from Main Street, it felt . . . different. More open. Less pressing in on him. It was a strange feeling. Tucker had always said that "wide open spaces" wasn't just a saying in his home state, but even though he'd been here before on a couple of research trips, Jackson hadn't truly realized what he'd meant. Until now.

He'd also assumed Tris stayed here, instead of returning to her native California, because David had been a born and bred Texan, and the memories were too strong, too important, for her to leave. But now he was beginning to wonder if there was more to it than that.

It was a chilly—by Texas standards—morning, only 56°, according to the thermometer hanging on the porch post, so he was glad he'd pulled on his black canvas jacket. He only planned on walking around a bit, just to look, so he'd be back before it got as warm as the clear blue sky suggested it would. The clear blue sky he was thankful for, since it made his sunglasses a bit less conspicuous.

He settled his baseball cap on his head as he stood in front of Tris's half of the duplex, one in a row of three arrayed along what he gathered was Bluebonnet Lane, where it crossed Hickory. He started to map out his exploration. And through all his plans was the hope that he would be pretty much unnoticed. Although if small-town gossip was as efficient as he'd heard it was, that might be too much to ask. Maybe he should just hope to be ignored.

He could see the park Tris had talked about and headed that way, although he thought he'd check it out after he'd managed to find that bakery she'd raved about. He wanted to buy a box full of something to thank her for the great breakfast she'd fixed this morning. He'd make that his last stop, though, after he'd figured out the town layout.

That decided, he crossed Hickory and headed toward Main Street. Across from the park was a cluster of buildings of varying sizes, mostly stone, and one built from what appeared to be the same kind of stone as the saloon Jeremy had been so fascinated with. When he saw the small sign in front, indicating it was the Last Stand Police Department, he smiled at the juxtaposition.

He took a moment to orient himself, realizing the large, two-story building up on the corner was the library because he could see the back of the statue from here. The relative size of the buildings made him smile again; that the library was about three times the size of the police department seemed significant.

As he passed the sidewalk that led to the single-story building, a man was coming down it, away from the building. Tall, maybe even an inch or so taller than him, with dark hair under a black felt cowboy hat. And Jackson immediately had the feeling no one would ever dare contest the man's right to wear it. He had the look and stride of a genuine cowboy. But there was something else about him, something about the way he scanned the area around him that—

He reached the end of the walkway just before Jackson got there. He turned just slightly, obviously to check out the newcomer, and as he moved, Jackson spotted the badge on his belt beneath his jacket. Detective, in plain clothes,

Jackson guessed. But then the man stopped, looked him up and down, and proved him utterly wrong.

"Heard you were in town," the man said. Jackson blinked. Already? He wasn't sure what had shown in his face, but the man smiled as if he'd heard the unspoken thought. "From my sister-in-law, Joey."

Jackson relaxed. "Librarian Joey?" Then he put it together and realized this was no detective. Instinctively, he pulled off the masking sunglasses, thinking this was someone he should meet eye to eye. "You're . . . Chief Highwater?"

"Yes." There was no arrogance or sense of superiority coming from the man, just a cool, capable competence. "I didn't realize until my wife told me that Mrs. Carhart is your sister."

So, he didn't read or watch gossip. That was encouraging. "Yes. She is."

"Her husband was a very respected man in Last Stand."

"Rightfully so," Jackson said, meaning it.

Highwater nodded. "Joey also said you were here because you're worried about your son."

It was too true for him to resent the fact that Joey had told him. He had that kind of relationship with Tris. She'd shared everything with him, even about people he didn't even know. Which told him what he'd already suspected about Joey Highwater was true. Still, he hesitated to pour his guts out to even this man.

"He's with Tris now, out at the Baylor ranch. Ms. Baylor

offered to let him spend time with her horses."

"Nic is good that way." Chief Highwater looked at him as if he completely understood the deflection. "I've got a son myself," the man went on quietly. "Six months old now. I'm starting to understand that kind of worry."

Jackson let out a breath. If this was the man's approach, he must get people to confess all kinds of things. "He . . . wasn't doing well, after his mother died."

The other man studied him for a moment, and all Jackson could think was that he was glad he hadn't done anything illegal, because those piercing eyes didn't look like they ever missed a thing.

"Wasn't?" the man finally said, very quietly.

Only then did Jackson realize he'd used the past tense. And he couldn't help smiling. "Yeah. He's already doing better, since we got here."

The police chief smiled back, and it was more genuine than just about any smile he saw back home. "Glad to hear it. Welcome to Last Stand, Mr. Thorpe. Call on us if you need us. Now, if you'll excuse me, I have rounds to make."

Jackson blinked again as he watched the man head toward Main Street. Rounds? The Last Stand Chief of Police what, walked a beat? Okay, that was different. Very different. And as he watched, he caught himself thinking he could do a lot worse than to model Austin Holt more on this man than the imaginary cowboy that lived in his head.

And as he stood there, watching the man go, he had the

feeling yet again that coming here just might have been the smartest thing he'd ever done. But that also reminded him he didn't have to worry about how he portrayed the fictional rancher any longer.

He'd been ignoring Miles's calls since that day at the beach in front of his house. And those from Felix Swiff, the show's chief executive producer, even longer. The only person he'd talked to was Tucker, and that was because the man had backed him all the way, even though it could affect his own career, since most of his work was doubling Jackson.

You go soak up some Texas spirit. Both you and Jeremy. You'll be the better for it.

Apparently, he was right. Because he was already feeling it. Feeling as if there was hope, as if Jeremy might also find that feeling here, or at the least be distracted enough to loosen his grip on the pain he kept clinging to. He was self-aware enough to realize that were it not for worrying about his son, he'd likely be in the same place. But he'd had to tamp down his own pain to a dull ache to deal with Jeremy's ripping need.

Which had also meant Austin Holt had to die. Or whatever they were going to do to write him out of the show. He hoped, fiercely, that it would go on without him, not only because he knew millions of viewers loved it, but because everybody on the crew worked so damned hard to make it the success it had become. He didn't want to be the one to put an end to that, to put them out of work in a cutthroat industry. Then again, *Stonewall* had been such a success, it might be easier for them now.

He shook off the feelings of guilt and started walking. He looked at the statue again when he reached the corner, and that chance meeting unrolled in his mind's eye all over again. He shook that off, too, and turned the opposite way.

There was a wine-tasting room on the corner, and he remembered Tris telling him the Hill Country was rapidly becoming wine country. He could see why—the terrain and weather seemed like it would suit. Next came a row of three connected buildings, and the first one made him smile just with the name. Yippee Ki Yay was the perfect tag for a western store. And at a glance in the front window, he saw several things he could picture Ms. Baylor wearing. He paused at the front door, looking at the sign that portrayed a cowboy on a wildly bucking horse, which made him think of Tucker and his aborted bull riding career. He'd asked him once if he missed it.

"The thrill, the competition? Yeah, sort of." He'd grinned that Tucker grin. "The aches and pains, not so much."

He kept walking, knowing without having to see any signage that he had reached the bakery. Those appetite-awakening smells were unmistakable. He seriously thought about going in now, but he wanted to continue his tour of Main Street, and if he went in there now, he'd probably only have an empty bag to take back to Tris's place. He jammed his hands into the pockets of his jeans to remind himself he didn't want to lug around a full bag, anyway.

He smiled at the next shop, another bakery, but this one apparently for pets, offering an array of dog biscuits, cat treats, and birdseed delicacies that boggled him.

Across the next street was a large church, with enough people clustered in the courtyard even on this Saturday to make him want to steer clear. So he crossed Main Street there and found himself in front of a store called Last Stand Expeditions, which he gathered sold supplies and had information on local hiking and river trips. He made a note of that as well, thinking Jeremy might like that too. The last time they'd visited, the three of them alive and well, Tris had taken them down to New Braunfels to see Gruene Hall, the state's oldest still-functioning dance hall, which had hosted many a major music star, and launched a few more. They'd taken a walk down by the Guadalupe River, and Jeremy had been especially intrigued by the people floating along on large inner tubes.

He added that to the list. If, of course, he could ever get him away from that pony. He continued walking, past a restaurant with a large outdoor patio, then crossed Hickory again and glanced in the window of another bakery of sorts, this one with apparently any kind of pie you could imagine. Tris loved lemon meringue, and there happened to be one in the case he could see from out here, so he added that to the list. The list that was surprising him with its length. He'd never really thought about spending a lot of time in a small town in Texas, but now that he was, he was finding a lot more he might like to do, and more importantly, that Jeremy might like to do, than he'd ever expected.

Next door to the pie shop was a place that stopped him dead. A newspaper? An actual small-town newspaper? Did they even exist anymore? *The Defender.* Interesting name. He wondered if it had something to do with that last stand the place was named for. He came up even with some clippings posted in the front window, one of which included the masthead of the paper, and he knew he was right, because the image above the name was a drawing of the saloon that was just a bit farther on across the street.

A movement inside caught his eye, and he looked through the window to see a lovely auburn-haired woman talking to an older, gray-haired man. They were both smiling, and then the man nodded and turned to go into the office behind him, with the words EDITOR IN CHIEF, *THE DEFENDER* painted on the glass in the door. The woman turned and headed toward the outer door, just to his right. She smiled brightly at him as she came out. He thought he saw a glint of recognition in her expression, but she said only, "Nice day for a walk around town. Enjoy."

He stared after her as she went. How had she known that was what he was doing?

He started to continue that walk when something posted in the window caught his eye, a story that looked as if it had been up there for a while, a story about a terrorist threat that had been averted by the sheer courage of a man who stopped a suicide bomber, fully believing he would die himself in the effort.

Then Police Lieutenant Shane Highwater.

He remembered the second plaque on the statue, commemorating more heroics from the man. *No wonder he's the chief now. And no wonder you picked up that rock-solid feel radiating from him.*

That was the kind of genuine courage Hollywood could only imitate.

Chapter Twelve

"SO HE REALLY just up and walked away?" Nic heard Tris's sigh as she kept watching her nephew on the pinto pony. "So it seems."

"What happens now? On the show, I mean?"

The star's sister shrugged. "I gather they're trying to decide what to do. To kill off the character, or leave a door open." She grimaced. "He did kind of dump this on them without notice. I know he feels bad about that, but he was afraid for Jeremy."

"And that trumped everything?"

"And anything," Tris agreed. Then, in a tone of aggravation, she went on. "I just get so angry at all those bloggers and internet geniuses who think they know why, that it was some actor-y thing, some 'clash of vision' kind of thing. Because an actor couldn't really walk away from the one thing they're all obsessed about, a big hit, for the sake of someone else, even his own child."

She gave Nic a sideways look, and there was a bit of color in her cheeks. And her tone was calmer when she said, "Sorry. It's just that I know he's been in such anguish over

Jeremy, so much that he's barely dealt with his own grief. He truly loved Leah, always said she was what kept him sane and balanced."

"Don't apologize for feeling strongly," Nic said as she felt an inward twinge. Because there had been a time when her mother had told her almost the same thing about her father. *He's kept me from going crazy, given me the strength to keep fighting. I don't know what I would have done without him.*

She'd never considered that the man she'd thought of as a guy pretending to be someone he's not was also a human being with real, genuine feelings powerful enough to make him walk away from a career-making part. Especially a guy who'd been a virtual unknown before he'd stepped into the skin of a character named Austin Holt.

"Jeremy is having such fun. It's absolutely wonderful to see after all this time," Tris said.

"I'm glad."

"It's the pony, I think. Jackson has tried to get him to ride with him when he goes on trail rides, but I think Jeremy was intimidated by a full-sized horse."

That surprised her. "Your brother actually rides voluntarily? When not on camera?"

Tris gave her a sideways look. Nic sensed her hesitation, realized the probable cause; she didn't want to anger the person letting Jeremy do what was making him so happy. "Don't worry about slapping me down. I probably have it coming. I admit to being a bit . . . prejudiced against Hollywood."

"Well, that's the first step to overcoming it," Tris said, smiling now.

Nic smiled wryly. "Seems like one I need to take, at least in this case."

Tris's smile widened. "In answer to your question, yes, Jackson rides a lot. He loves it, and the horses, and has ever since his friend Tucker got him started when he got him his first job on a film crew, helping wrangle the animals for a movie. That was where Miles Flint first spotted him, helping that horse."

Helping?

. . . go look at how Jackson Thorpe was, as they say, discovered.

Her mother's words came back to her. Obviously, the story must be well-known, since the man's sister seemed to be assuming she'd know it. But she didn't. She'd always had the idea he'd just been swept up out of nowhere and plopped into the role that had morphed into being the lynchpin of one of the biggest television hits ever.

She felt more than a little embarrassed now at her assumption he'd never done a lick of actual hard work to get where he was. She'd remembered her mother telling her about how some famous golden age actress had been "discovered" sitting at a lunch counter, and figured some agent or other had taken one look at Thorpe's admittedly gorgeous face and body and said, "There's my guy!"

She'd made a lot of assumptions about the man, and they were falling apart one by one. Which made her start wondering why she had, so far, been so wrong. True, she'd only had his Hollywood image—and her own feelings about such things—to base it on, but still, it wasn't like her to . . . well, to judge like this.

Maybe she needed to quit thinking about Jackson Thorpe and do a little work on Nicole Baylor.

JACKSON HAD CONTINUED his walking tour after his encounter with the chief, an encounter that had made him think of stopping to speak to the man's brother. The saloonkeeper. A juxtaposition that still made him smile.

He'd gone into the saloon, and the man—Slater, he said to call him—had asked if he wanted a drink, on the house.

"As Tris's brother," he said pointedly. "Not as the big star."

He grimaced. "Neither guy ever drinks before dark, and then not much. He crashed and burned once, at the worst possible time, and is making sure it never happens again."

The other Highwater brother studied him for a moment, then nodded. "Hang on a sec," he'd said, and disappeared into the back. He came out with something that looked almost slushy, an odd shade of yellow orange in a tall, frosty glass with a straw.

"It's better when the peaches are in season and it's fresh, but I keep some frozen on hand most of the time."

Peaches? Jackson took a sip, and the flavor practically burst over his tongue. "Wow. That's amazing."

Slater grinned at him. "Local peaches make all the difference."

"I never thought of Texas as peach-growing country."

"Nobody did, until somebody did."

That made him laugh. And he realized it wasn't just Jeremy who had relaxed here; he'd laughed more himself since they'd arrived than he had in the last three years.

They'd begun talking about him staying a while and needing a car. Slater suggested a dealer over in Fredericksburg that also leased vehicles. That, Jackson greatly appreciated, but when the man pulled out a phone to call someone who could give him a ride there, he was a little stunned.

"Isn't there a taxi or ride share or something?" he asked.

"A couple, but only a couple, and they're usually pretty busy. Besides, it's only about twelve miles, and I know just the person. My sister-in-law. She has today off, since my brother Sean and his wife are watching their son today." He grinned. "Elena can't help herself when it comes to babies."

"I'm sure she's got better things to do—"

"Than give Jackson Thorpe a ride? I doubt it. But fair warning, she used to be a reporter."

His long-conditioned wariness sprang to life. "Used to

be?"

Slater nodded. "Now she just does human-interest stuff. So I can't say she won't ask questions, but she won't be pushing you for a gossip column or anything. She's not a small-picture kind of woman."

He made the call before Jackson could stop him, and he couldn't see any way out of it after that. And when the woman walked into the saloon, he realized he should have guessed; it was the woman he'd seen coming out of the newspaper office.

It only belatedly hit him that Slater had said his sister-in-law. And he'd looked at the saloonkeeper, who was nonchalantly drying a glass. "Which brother?" he asked dryly.

"I think you already guessed."

"The police chief is married to a reporter?"

"Ex-reporter." The woman's voice was cheery as she came up behind him. "I don't do news anymore. Kind of a conflict of interest when you're married to one of the biggest newsmakers in the county."

He remembered the story he'd seen in the window of the paper. "And one of the biggest heroes?"

The look that came across her face then made his throat tighten. It was so full of not just love, but admiration and respect. Leah had looked at him that way, even when he didn't deserve it, when they'd been struggling just to get by. She'd never, ever given up on him.

"Yes," she said simply. "Lily Highwater," she added,

holding out a hand.

He took it, just for a moment. "Look, you don't need to—"

"I have an errand in Fredericksburg I've been putting off, so you'll actually be doing me a favor by making me do it."

"I…thank you."

And so he ended up in a car with the chief of police's wife, who happened to be a writer of human-interest stories. He'd expected a barrage of questions, but Slater hadn't lied. She didn't push. At all. It didn't take him long to figure out that Joey hadn't told only her husband about his situation. Or her husband had told his brother, who had told his wife. But back home, his situation wouldn't have stopped any reporter, ex or otherwise, from grabbing this chance to batter him with prying inquiries. In fact, it would have resulted in even more pressure, more paparazzi hiding behind every tree and bush and wall, hoping to catch a shot of either him or Jeremy in some kind of emotional state of trauma.

But Lily Highwater hadn't. She'd asked only one question, after a few minutes in silence as they worked their way out to the highway that would take them to Fredericksburg. She'd glanced at him and said honestly, "As a new mother myself, I greatly respect anyone who would do this for their child, Mr. Thorpe. I know who the nexus of the local grapevine is, and if I tell him to put the word out on *why* you're here, I can promise ninety percent of Last Stand will back off and give you the room and time to see to your son.

Shall I do it?"

"In exchange for what?"

She gave him another glance, her expression almost sad now. "Is everything a trade-off in that town?"

He didn't have to ask what town she meant. "Pretty much."

"Well, this is Last Stand, Texas, Mr. Thorpe. And I give you my word we're not that way."

He didn't know what to say. Finally, with a sideways look at her as she drove, he asked, "Is that a word with your husband's position behind it?"

She didn't deny it. "If necessary. To borrow a cliché, his word is law in Last Stand."

"I can see why," he said, thinking again of that story in the window, and the plaque on the statue.

"So, yes or no, Mr. Thorpe?"

He took a deep breath. It was all in or get out of the pool, as Tucker was wont to say. "Yes. On one condition."

"What's that?"

"Stop calling me Mr. Thorpe."

She laughed, and it was a lovely sound. And he had the feeling that Shane Highwater had found a woman worthy of him. Which was saying something.

Last Stand was indeed a different town than Hollywood. And that could only be a good thing.

Too bad the woman he had to deal with was Nicole Baylor.

Chapter Thirteen

. . . GO LOOK AT how Jackson Thorpe was, as they say, discovered.

Nic was pouring over her message board, looking at the discussion threads she usually not just ignored but avoided. It was almost stunning to realize how much chatter there was about a TV show on this site supposedly dedicated to horses.

It took her a while to find the specific threads, since it had been mostly discussed back at the start of the show nearly five years ago. But someone linked to a news story, and she chose that to get the non-fan version. Or at least something that pretended not to be. But she had to admit after reading the story of one of the horses on a film in which Thorpe had been a wrangler and a background player, she felt . . . impressed again. First of all, it reminded her he was close friends with stuntman Tucker Culhane, the man she remembered as a rodeo champion here in Texas from some years ago.

But the story focused mainly on how, on location, a horse had been spooked and ran into a mud flat and been up to his withers fast. It had been Thorpe who had risked himself to go out there and keep the horse's head above the surface, yelled out some orders to the others on the scene, and then dived down to put a strap around the animal's ribs so the truck on dry land could pull him free. The panicked creature had initially kicked out, until Thorpe calmed him, and it was only the next day it was learned he had acquired a couple of cracked ribs in the process.

She found a phone video of the incident, and despite wondering about the mindset of someone who would stand by and do nothing but record, she found it mesmerizing. Jackson Thorpe may have been just a bit player on this production, but in this rescue, he'd been the star. Miles Flint had been there to see the whole thing and had decided then and there that he had the hero of his pet project, a modern-day western, to take advantage of the streaming culture that had developed.

"I just told Jackson I wanted him to take the man who saved that horse and put him on the screen," Flint had said. "And he did."

Nic went back to the original article and sat there staring at the photos, one a mud-encrusted figure who, because she knew, she could tell was hunched slightly to protect those ribs. The other was him in character on set, looking into the distance against a darkening blue sky the color of his eyes. The image made those eyes pop in the picture, but in person they were even . . . more. He was clad much as he had been today, in serviceable clothes, only with the inevitable cowboy hat, pulled down at the perfect angle to even further emphasize those eyes.

The hat don't make you a cowboy.

She could hear her father's voice in her head and couldn't stop herself from grinning. No, putting on the hat didn't make you cowboy, no matter how good it made you look. And she freely admitted her personal bias was pretty strong. She didn't mind Texans who wore them when they had nothing to do with the work that had inspired the headgear, it was almost state-approved attire. It was the outsiders she was . . . okay, prejudiced against. Not in a nasty, name-calling way, but in requiring them to prove themselves before she'd give them the respect she'd give someone who did the work it implied.

No, the hat didn't make anyone a cowboy.

But what Jackson Thorpe had done to save that horse just might.

"Where'd you get the car?"

Jackson looked at Jeremy, marveling at how even this simple question made him ache a little inside, but unlike the last two years, in a very, very good way. Because not so long ago, the question wouldn't have occurred, or if it had, it would have taken too much of the boy's emotional energy to ask.

"Remember the man who told us to go see Joey at the

library?"

"The guy in the building with the bullet holes?"

Jackson smiled and nodded. "That's him. I stopped by to thank him for sending us there, and he told me where I could rent a car. Since we're going to be here a while, I figured we needed one. We can't borrow your aunt Tris's all the time."

Jeremy had gone very still. Jackson immediately ran what he'd said back through his mind, searching for something he'd said wrong. Was it about not borrowing Tris's car? Was he afraid this was somehow distancing them from his beloved aunt?

Finally, Jeremy said in a tiny voice, "We're staying?"

That voice was so small he couldn't even tell if it was with fear or hope. "I thought you wanted to," he said carefully. "But if you'd rather—"

"I want to stay! I didn't think you would." Then, after a moment, he asked, "Don't you have to go back to work?"

Jackson drew in a deep breath as he realized he actually hadn't told Jeremy the whole truth yet. He'd only told him they were going to visit Tris.

He pulled off Main Street and into the parking lot of what was as close to a strip mall as he'd seen in Last Stand. There were parking spaces in front of the businesses, most of which appeared to be medical offices, but he left those alone and parked some distance out. He turned off the engine, then turned to look at his son. Even as he did, he saw fear enter the boy's eyes, as if he was afraid of what was coming before Jackson even said it.

Why wouldn't he be? You were the one who had to tell him his mother was dead.

Jeremy hadn't even understood what dead meant at the time, he was so young. Jackson wasn't sure he understood it even now, although the idea of never seeing her again was obviously creeping in.

It had taken a long time to convince the child it wasn't something he had done that was making his mother stay away. The doctor they'd gone to had told him that was typical, normal. Just as it was normal that the then five-year-old didn't have the words to describe how he was feeling, and Jackson would need to help him with that. And normal that the boy didn't understand the concept of forever.

And all Jackson had been able to think at the time was that there wasn't a damned thing about any of this that was normal. But there was one thing Jeremy needed to understand, one thing he needed to be certain of. That while he might only have one parent left, that parent loved him completely.

"I'm not going back to work," he said.

Jeremy stared at him, brow furrowed in puzzlement. "Huh?"

He took in a breath and said firmly, "There is nothing in my life more important than you. And right now, we need to be together. We have to make a life without your mom,

Jeremy, and I don't think we can do it back home. We've tried for two years now, and it's not working."

His son was staring at him now, wide-eyed. "I don't understand. Are we going to . . . live here now?"

"I don't know," he admitted. "But I thought we'd stay for a while and see if we like it."

His focus on the "we" seemed to be working, because Jeremy calmed a little. "Stay with Aunt Tris?"

"For a while," he repeated. "But we should look for a place for us too."

Jeremy lowered his gaze, but then gave him a sideways look. "What about school?"

"We'll figure that out."

"Aunt Tris is a teacher," the boy said.

Jackson found himself smiling rather crookedly at the almost sly note in that observation. "Yes. Yes, she is, and we can talk to her about what to do about getting your royal smartness back to learning. You've got some catching up to do."

He wasn't really worried a lot about that. He knew Jeremy was a very smart kid, and he was already ahead of most others his age in reading and math, and probably other things too.

Like the hard realities of life. And death.

After another moment of silence, Jeremy asked, "Where're we going?"

Jackson hesitated, then decided to risk the joke. "You

mean you don't want to go into that doctor's office over there?"

Jeremy's eyes widened as he looked the direction Jackson had nodded. "No! I don't wanna go there. I'm not sick. I'm just . . . sad."

Jackson thought his heart was going to shatter. "I know," he said, barely able to manage a whisper. "So am I."

His son's gaze snapped back to his face. "You still miss her?"

He reached out then, because it felt like the only thing to do. The therapist had told him it would take many repetitions of the same answer to convince the boy. He clasped Jeremy's shoulders in both hands and gently squeezed as he said, letting the ache he always felt into his voice, "I will always miss her, Jeremy. Always."

That declaration of shared pain soothed the boy, at least to where he nodded as he blinked back the sudden tears Jackson knew all too well.

"So, where are we going?"

Sensing the moment had passed, Jackson shrugged. "Your aunt had some papers to grade, so I thought we'd just drive around a little, look at stuff."

"Okay." He sounded interested enough. But then he asked, "Can we go back to Nic's? I really want to ride Pie again."

He should have expected that. Cautiously, he said, "Eventually. But it's Sunday, so I think we give Pie the day off, okay?" *And me the day off from dealing with the woman who, if she doesn't hate me, doesn't like me much.*

"Oh. Okay."

The boy seemed to accept that easily enough. As he pulled out of the parking lot and back onto Main Street, Jackson had the thought that the conversation they'd just had would never have happened back home. And that alone told him this had been the right thing to do.

They drove past the library and the statue, and Jeremy asked if they could go back and see Joey again. Jackson immediately agreed to that. They went by the courthouse and then, across the street, the saloon. He smiled inwardly at the juxtaposition again, wondering if it was intentional. They stopped at the park and walked around, and at the south side, he saw Jeremy looking across the street at the elementary and middle schools that faced it. The boy didn't speak, but Jackson couldn't help thinking that he was wondering what it would be like to go to school here.

Finally, he pulled in behind the western wear store. Jeremy stared at the sign at the back entrance, which portrayed a saddle bronc rider aboard a horse in full buck, completely airborne.

"Is that what Uncle T used to do?" Jeremy asked, a little wide eyed.

"Yes, but on a bull and without a saddle," he answered. "Even scarier."

"I'm glad he doesn't do that anymore."

"So's his entire body," Jackson said. "So, what do you say we go in and get you some Texas-style stuff?"

Jeremy lit up, something he rarely did anymore, and Jackson was grateful once more for the impulse that had brought them here.

"Could I get some cowboy boots? Nic said it's easier to ride in them."

"I think we can manage that," he said, his voice a little gruff because his throat had tightened up on him again.

"Welcome to Last Stand, you two!"

The woman just coming out of the western wear store smiled broadly at them, but somewhat to Jackson's surprise, left it at that and continued on her way. He liked that she'd included Jeremy, though.

In fact, everyone they'd encountered today seemed to be in the same mode—acknowledge, but don't intrude. Apparently Lily Highwater had been right about the Last Stand grapevine, both in its speed and responsiveness to a Highwater request.

"People are nicer here."

Jeremy's quiet statement as they went into the store was unusual. The boy usually didn't comment on things like that. And Jackson couldn't argue with the truth of it, he just didn't like thinking that it was so noticeable, even to a seven-year-old. Or that his son had been at the mercy of too many not-so-nice people. Not that he'd ever been mistreated, but Jeremy was very good at sensing sincerity. Or the lack thereof. Probably better than he was.

The people of Last Stand seemed completely sincere to him, and Jeremy apparently agreed. He was beginning to think there was something to the old small-town warmth vs. big-city chill debate. And in that moment, he was very glad they'd left Hollywood behind.

Chapter Fourteen

OKAY, THIS WAS crazy.

She missed him. The kid had only been here twice, and she missed him. Missed seeing him so happy, and the look of relief and joy on his aunt's face—or okay, his father's—as they watched him.

Or maybe it was just that she'd had a restless night and so had gotten up early and had all her chores for the day done by ten. Then she'd ridden over to Clark's old house, which they periodically checked on simply because it went against the Baylor grain to just let it go. And besides, she loved the place, the simplicity of it, and most of all the location, atop a rise with a view out over the hills, toward the creek that ran across the northwest corner of the ranch in the distance. A view that she wished the main house had.

The place had been well built and was in good shape. All she'd had to do was dust a little, run some water to check the pipes, and flip on the circuit breaker to make sure the power still worked. That, plus cleaning the windows, and she was done, and it was still only eleven.

That left her too much time to think. That was all that

"missing the kid" feeling was.

She thought about taking Sass out for a run, but this was his relax day, and the most she generally asked of him on Sunday was to happily roam the big pasture and roll in the dirt as he so liked to do. It meant a bath for him later, but she didn't mind that because the horse enjoyed it so much, and would play with the water, most often trying to spray it back on her.

She slipped a halter on Pie and led him out to the corral attached to the barn. He was small enough that that was plenty of room for him to romp in. And he needed to work off the energy that never seemed to fade. As she watched the pony kick up his heels, she found herself back on the original thought she was trying to avoid, wondering if Jeremy would come back. If his father would let him.

Wondering if his father would bring him.

She owed him an apology. Not that she was in a hurry to do it. It would be awkward and embarrassing, but she owed it, and she would do it.

She'd gone back and watched that video of him saving the mired horse again. A couple of times. There was no denying the heroic effort he'd made. No denying that he'd been the only one there who'd even tried.

No denying how utterly hot he looked doing it.

So, you joining the Jackson Thorpe fan club now?

No, she told herself. She was just dropping out of the hate-him-on-sight club.

She heard the wheels on the path her father had built and turned to see her mother heading for her. She handled the chair with the ease of long practice, and Nic wasn't really kidding when she joked that she'd put Mom's arm strength up against any hand on the ranch.

"How is he doing?" her mother asked without preamble.

"Fine," Nic said. "I think he enjoyed being back under saddle. It's been a while."

"I can see Pie is fine. I meant," her mother said rather pointedly, "the little boy."

"Oh." Nic felt a touch of heat in her cheeks. If her mother ever ventured one of her rare criticisms, it was about her focus on the animals, to the exclusion of almost everything else.

Someday, Nicole, I'd like some grandchildren of the human variety.

She usually countered that unsubtle request with an offer to go pick up some guy at the Last Stand Saloon. A while back, her mother would have retorted she could do a lot worse than Slater Highwater, but now it was obvious that he and Joey were such a perfect match that no one could imagine either of them with anyone else.

She gave herself an inward shake. "His aunt says he's doing better since they've come to Last Stand than he has since his mother was killed."

Barbara Baylor nodded as if not at all surprised. "This is a good place. By the way"—Nic tensed, because that phrase from her mother usually signaled an incoming salvo—"I ran into Lily and Shane Highwater in town this morning."

"With the baby, I'm sure?" she asked dryly, figuring they'd be back to that.

"Of course." Her mother's smile widened. "That man is going to be a wonderful father. But Lily mentioned she drove Jackson Thorpe to Fredericksburg yesterday, to pick up a rental car."

Nic blinked. "Lily did?"

"Slater called her, since he knew she had planned to go to the library there anyway, to look at some historical documents for a piece she's writing."

"Oh." She wasn't sure what she was supposed to say, so said nothing.

"Don't you see what that means?" her mother asked, sounding as impatient as she ever got, which wasn't much. If her accident had taught her nothing else, it was patience.

"No, what?"

"If he's renting a car, they're staying. For a while at least."

"Oh." Now she felt silly, because that was all she could come up with.

"And," her mother added, "she said he agreed to let her tell Mr. Diaz why he was here, which of course will activate the grapevine."

She blinked as the image of the feedstore owner formed in her mind. He told Lily to tell the biggest gossip in town?

That surprised her, but she supposed it shouldn't have. She'd been foolish to think he truly wanted a low profile here. He was a Hollywood star. Of course he wanted the word out, so he—

"Lily, of course, made it clear to him that he needed to include the reason Jackson was here, for the sake of his little boy, and for everyone to back off and let them alone. Or at least treat them like anyone else in town. And you know not even Samuel Diaz is going to cross Lily Highwater."

She couldn't help it, she laughed. "No, he wouldn't. Lily would write a profile of him that would run him out of town in embarrassment. Not to mention Shane would want a word or two with him."

"Exactly." Her mother gave her a sideways look. "So, when is he coming back?"

"Want to be sure you're here?" she teased.

"It will give me something to talk about at the next Daughters of LS meeting," Mom said, and she was grinning.

Emotion flooded Nic, that this strong, indomitable woman was her mother. "I love you, Mom. And I really don't know if he's coming back. I hope so, for Jeremy's sake. It was good for him."

"I love you, too, Nicky." The grin flashed again, lighting up warm brown eyes. "Just let me know when you do find out, okay?"

"What if Jeremy's coming with his aunt again?"

"Still let me know. She sounds like someone I'd like to

meet."

Nic nodded. "I really like her."

"Good enough for me. It's the one you don't like I disagree with."

"Yeah, well," Nic muttered. "I'm rethinking that. He really does love that boy."

"And you thought he wasn't capable of that?"

"I thought he was an actor."

"Even in his personal life?"

"I guess so," she admitted. It sounded pretty silly out loud.

But then, a lot of her assumptions about Jackson Thorpe seemed a bit silly right now.

It was Nic's turn to fix dinner that night, and since she was in no mood—okay, she was too distracted—she instead went into town to pick up their favorite meal from Valencia's, the best Tex-Mex restaurant in town, if not the county. She clearly wasn't the only one with the same idea this Sunday night, because there were three other people ahead of her when she arrived. One was Hannah Roberts, one of the sales staff at Yippee Ki Yay, who greeted her with a smile.

"Well, here she is, the topic of much conversation in the store today."

Nic blinked. "What?"

"Had a certain . . . very famous customer today, with a little boy who couldn't stop talking about you." Her voice dropped to a whisper. "I'd mention the name, but word is out to be hush-hush."

So the Last Stand grapevine was alive, well-oiled, and functioning according to command. But that realization was nothing compared to Hannah's pronouncement that she had been a topic of conversation.

"You're going to explain, I presume," she said dryly.

Hannah did, and the account of the famous star buying a pair of cowboy boots for his little boy, along with a pearl-snap shirt and a bandana—"Pretty much anything he wanted," Hannah said—made her smile.

"I tried to talk him into a new hat, or a pair of boots for himself, but he wasn't having any of it. They were here for Jeremy, he said. But you know the best part?"

Not until you tell me. She knew this was part of Hannah's makeup. She just loved to gossip, but in her own, hold back the best part until the end, way. "What?" she asked, playing along.

"He put back the Stetson I handed him and said he knew he had no business pretending to be a cowboy here, where so many real ones live."

Nic blinked. *The hat don't make you a cowboy . . .*

"He said that?" she finally got out.

"He did. You know, I've always liked him, and I love the show, but that was . . . a wonderful thing to say."

"Yes," Nic said. "Yes, it was."

"And I'm jealous. He's already been to your place and stayed the whole afternoon."

"Yes," she said, but what he'd said about the hat was still rocketing around in her brain.

"I went back and read about his wife's accident after they left. So sad. I mean, we drive fast here, but they drive crazy. And just think, if it had been fifteen minutes later, Jeremy would have been in that car with her, since she was on her way to pick him up from school."

Nic's breath caught. She hadn't known that.

She hadn't known a lot of things, it seemed.

Chapter Fifteen

JACKSON SAT, STARING at his phone screen. It hadn't been hard to find the number. She did run a business, after all. And it had been that thought that had started his dilemma. Started the ricocheting of his brain as if it were a billiard ball he'd hit a little too hard.

She ran a business. Training horses. Not riders, horses. But she was obviously a very good rider herself, so would it be a huge step to train a rider? He supposed he could find an actual riding instructor, but Jeremy liked her. A lot, judging by the way he kept talking about her. And Pie. So the bottom line was he wanted Jeremy to be able to keep riding that pony. But it wasn't right to take up her time and use her livestock and not pay her back.

He started to dial, then stopped. Maybe he should figure out his approach first. For Jeremy's sake, he didn't want to piss her off and have her say no.

He let out a sour, self-directed chuckle. He'd gotten quite spoiled in the last five years. Back home, he never had to think much anymore about whether someone would take his call. Not like the early days, when he and Leah had gotten married and had Jeremy, while he worked on the fringes, and only got those jobs thanks to Tucker.

He liked to think he'd at least paid Tucker back a little by making them a package deal. Part of his contract was that if a stand-in was needed, Tucker would be his. And thanks to Leah's rather intense budgeting and clever investing, even if he had blown his career to bits now, they'd both be okay for a good long time.

He heard laughter from the living room, where his sister and Jeremy were watching a movie. Or rather rewatching, in Jeremy's case; he loved the series with the aliens and the smart-mouthed raccoon.

He should be out there with them, not sitting here in the guest room, staring at his stupid phone because he couldn't work up the nerve to make one simple phone call. All the people in his world, including beautiful women, who would be delighted to answer the phone and hear, "Hi, this is Jackson Thorpe," but here he sat, fixated on the phone number for a woman even more beautiful who just happened not to like him much.

Disgusted with himself, he got up, shoved the phone back into his jeans pocket, and headed toward the sound of the television. He paused in the hallway opening to the main room, his throat suddenly tight again, as had happened so many times since they'd come here. It had been only four days, but the change in his son was marked and obvious. Right now he sat on the couch, cuddled up against his aunt, laughing at a snappy comeback his favorite character had made.

This is why I do it. Because it's an escape some people desperately need.

He'd never really put it into so many words like that before, and he knew some would laugh at him for even thinking it. He didn't care. He wasn't out to change the world, he was in this business because sometimes people needed to forget about that world for a while. He had a knack for putting himself into a part in a believable way, and he used it.

Knack, my ass. You study like a crazy person, Thorpe, to figure out who your character is. That's why they listen to you when you say he'd never do that.

Tucker's words echoed in his memory, spoken the day that, to their shock, the director of the episode they were working on agreed with him and ordered a change in a fairly major scene.

"Wait, wait," Jeremy exclaimed excitedly. Jackson refocused and saw Tris had the remote control in her hand and was aiming it at the screen. "You have to see the scene in the middle of the credits."

He smiled at that and walked into the room. "Skipping the credits?" he asked his sister in a tone of mock outrage.

"Only because this is my third time through," she said dryly.

He laughed and sat down next to Jeremy, who was still

glued to the screen, awaited the admittedly funny outtake they'd put halfway through. When it finally did actually end, Tris suggested ice cream for all, and Jeremy agreed with some enthusiasm. Another change for the better, since the boy's appetite usually required a lot of coaxing, to the point where he was at the bottom end of the scale of what he should weigh for his height and age.

"Oh, by the way," Tris said as she came back with three bowls of their unanimous fave, rocky road, and Jeremy dug in fast, "I presume you'd be available to take Jeremy out to the Baylors' tomorrow?"

He blinked. Sat there with the spoonful he'd just taken melting in his mouth. Swallowed it hastily. "What?"

"I called to see if they'd be okay with it."

"You did?" The image of himself sitting in the other room, staring at his phone screen, shot through his mind. And here Tris had simply done it. Done what he hadn't been able to do. Which, in a tangled way, said a lot more about him than her.

Tris tilted her head to look at him in that way that warned him she knew her brother all too well.

"And they said it was okay," Jeremy exclaimed excitedly. "But I have to go to bed on time, so I'll have lots of energy to ride Pie tomorrow." With that the boy gobbled the last bite of his ice cream, scrambled down from the couch, and headed for the hallway and the bathroom. A moment later he heard water running as the boy brushed his teeth.

"Mrs. Baylor answered," Tris said. "I'd always heard about her, but never actually talked to her before."

"From what Ms. Baylor told me, she's quite something," he said, as neutrally as he could manage and, he hoped, without any emphasis on the formal name. "Adapting, never giving up."

"Yes. But we talked more about the fact that she's a private tutor."

Jackson drew back slightly. "She is?"

"She was a teacher here at the middle school before her mishap—that's what she calls what most would say was a disaster—but she said she finds she likes working with individual students much better." Tris gave a wry smile. "I can see the appeal."

He knew she had days when dealing with a roomful of kids felt overwhelming. But she was good at it, and he knew it was what had gotten her through the worst part of her grief after David had died. He, on the other hand . . . He tried to remember where she had been at this point, two years after the fact. He couldn't really remember, but he knew it was likely better than how he was doing at that stage. Not that he hadn't accepted it had happened, but he wasn't handling it so well. If he had been, he would have brought Jeremy here a lot sooner, because the change in the boy in just days had been . . . well, remarkable.

"—do you think?"

He tuned back in, calling himself an idiot in his mind for

tuning out yet again. "What?"

Tris looked at him as if she knew exactly what had happened, but kindly only repeated her question. "If you're going to stay awhile, what do you think about having her tutor Jeremy? He's not middle school age yet, but he's smart enough, so it might be good for him. And she'd be willing to tailor a program for him."

"You already asked her?"

"With the understanding that it was up to you, of course. You said you thought you'd stay awhile, but if it's only awhile, then enrolling him in school here formally would be a problem. And he already wants to go there to ride, so I thought—"

"It's okay," he assured her. "And it sounds like the perfect solution." *Except for having to deal with Nicole Baylor regularly.*

"She's not cheap," his sister warned.

"Neither am I," he said with a wry smile.

"I know," Tris said softly. "You're always willing to pay people what they're worth. And more."

He shrugged. She rolled her eyes in that sisterly way of hers. "Anyway, you should talk with her tomorrow, see if you like her, and think it will work. And she said they could probably coordinate with some riding lessons for Jeremy, as a reward for hard work kind of thing."

That caught his attention. He certainly wasn't above that kind of bribery, if it got Jeremy back to caring about his learning, as he once had.

"And just think what an inspiration it would be for him, to see her get out of her wheelchair and onto a horse."

He blinked. Remembered the ramp and the pathway he'd seen, but it had never occurred to him that she could still mount a horse. "Her mother still rides?"

"She does, Nic says."

"Wow." He tried to ignore that the fact his sister was allowed to call her Nic ate at him a little.

"So you'll talk to her about it?"

"I think I'll talk to Jeremy first, but yes."

"Good call," Tris said with a wide smile.

He gathered up the empty ice cream bowls and carried them to the kitchen. He stood at the sink for a moment, wondering what he'd gotten himself into. Doubt flooded him, despite all his big promises. Was he really going to stay here long enough for all this?

"'Night, Dad."

The words turned him around, and when he did, his son threw his arms around him in an almost fierce hug. Something he hadn't really done on his own initiative in . . . two years.

The question that had been in his mind vanished. For this, he'd do anything.

Chapter Sixteen

"I OWE YOU an apology."

The man's eyes widened, as if those were words he'd never expected to hear. Or at least, never expected to hear from her. And that told her a little too much about how she'd been acting around him. It was embarrassing, how she'd let her presumptions dictate her actions, and she didn't like having to admit she'd done it. But she had, and she needed to make what amends she could.

Not only that, she wanted to get this out of the way fast, because she hated lugging around this twinge of guilt. She wasn't usually like this, and it was not a good feeling.

She heard a whoop from the boy riding the pony in the corral and glanced that way to be sure all was well. It was. Jeremy had really taken to riding and was learning fast. Even Pie acted as if he was having fun. The picture they made brought a smile back to her face and let her control those tangled emotions she was wrestling with.

When she looked back, she saw the man beside her had looked toward the sound as well. But she saw something else too. Saw that there'd been a relaxing of his tension as he watched his son. The love was still uppermost, but she hadn't realized quite how wound up he'd been until it had eased up a little. There was absolutely no doubt that he was also worried.

"He's a great kid," she said.

"Yes." It was barely a murmur, but she could still hear the emotion in it.

"And that's why I should have known."

He looked at her then. "Known what?"

"That a kid like that couldn't have the kind of man I assumed you were as a father."

He just stared at her, and suddenly she didn't have a clue what he was thinking. And so she stumbled on.

"I also talked to my friend Hannah, who works at Yippee Ki Yay. She told me what you said. About not wearing a cowboy hat." She smiled wryly. "One of my dad's favorite sayings, that I've heard since I was his"—she nodded toward Jeremy—"age is, 'The hat don't make you a cowboy.'"

He laughed, and it somehow sounded as wry as her voice had. "Truer words," he said.

"Hence the apology. I made some assumptions, including that you were the type who thought the opposite, that all you had to do was dress up and play the part, pretend to be a guy with a Texas name, to earn the title. And I'm sorry."

There, it was done. She'd said what she had to say. And he was still smiling. Sort of, although it looked a bit rueful now.

"Believe me," he said, "I know full well the difference between the fantasy and real ranch life, and that I'm ill-equipped to deal with the latter. I don't have the knowledge. Or, I suspect, the endurance."

That open, honest admission changed her relief after making the apology to gladness that she'd done it. In fact, if she were going to be honest with herself in turn, she'd admit that she found his openness about it rather . . . endearing. And that was something she never thought she'd be feeling about Jackson Thorpe, of all people.

"Ah, there you are."

Her mother's voice from behind them almost made her jump. Strangely, she hadn't even heard her approach. She was usually always tuned in for the sound of the chair on the track her father had built. She wasn't, however, surprised that her mother was here. She'd figured she wouldn't be able to resist the opportunity to meet the man.

As she often did when someone met her mother for the first time, she watched him for his first reaction to the woman in the chair. In a smooth, easy motion, he crouched down until they were at eye level. More points to him, since her mother hated when people bent over her.

And she knew from the glint in her mother's eye that she'd also noticed. And approved.

"Mrs. Baylor?"

Nic somehow liked that, too, that he didn't assume. "Mr. Thorpe," her mother said, smiling so widely, it pleased

Nic even more. She had to remember her mother was meeting someone famous that she admired.

But his next words startled her. "Am I late?"

"Not at all. I just finished my last session a little early."

"Good," he said with a crooked smile. "I'd hate to start off wrong-footed."

"You sound like you've had some experience with that."

"Sometime I'll tell you about my high school history teacher. The terror of the entire school district."

Mom laughed and looked up at Nic. "Sounds like Mrs. Valencia, doesn't it?"

"Yes," she said, acknowledging the now-retired teacher's ability to strike fear into anyone who took her subject lightly—but who'd also had the knack to inspire her students to greater heights than even they had ever imagined they could reach. Including her. She had gone from near-terror that first day to near the top of the class, to her own shock.

Mom turned back to the man she clearly admired. "Shall we go inside? I'm sure you'd like to see where it all happens. And we can discuss a plan."

"And payment, of course," he said, straightening up. And Nic noted he'd never wobbled or complained, just stayed in that crouch the entire time.

"What," she finally asked, "are you two talking about?"

"You didn't tell her?" Mom asked, looking at the man who was glancing once more at his son, who had stopped Pie for some apparently required patting of his neck.

He looked back. "We . . . hadn't gotten to that yet."

Nic sighed. "I was busy apologizing, Mom."

"Oh," her mother said. "Good. I'm sure you needed to." Then, briskly, she went on. "We're going to discuss my possibly tutoring Jeremy. Bring him in, in about a half an hour, will you?"

"I . . . sure." Her mother was going to tutor Jackson Thorpe's son? And this meeting had clearly been planned ahead of time. How had she missed this?

Too busy hating on the guy you didn't even know?

She started out watching them go back toward the house, but found herself appreciating the way he moved and the way his jeans fit a little too much, and turned around to watch Jeremy and Pie trotting around the corral.

When she took the boy inside at the requested half hour later—when it was officially work-related, and her mother said half an hour, that's what she meant—she found both of them laughing. And she noticed that when Jeremy saw his father laughing, he relaxed a little and smiled.

"Thank you, dear," Mom said.

"Come on in," Jackson—she was thinking of him that way now—said to the boy. "I think we've got a plan you'll like."

"I will?" the boy asked.

"It'll mean you have to come here every day during the week, though," his father said.

Jeremy lit up. "Really?"

He sounded so excited it warmed a part of Nic she rarely heard from, the part that occasionally thought about having kids to pass her love of this place and this life on to.

"It'll be like school, but you'll have it all to yourself. Mrs. Baylor's a teacher, like Aunt Tris, but she only takes one student at a time."

The boy looked at Mom a little warily. "Why?"

"It's more fun that way," Mom said, with that wide, warm smile that never seemed to fail to charm.

"Oh."

"Especially when there's a reward right away," she added.

"There is? What?" Jeremy asked.

"Riding lessons with my daughter."

The boy's gaze snapped to Nic. "You'll keep teaching me, so I can ride like that someday?"

Jeremy pointed to the framed photograph on the wall, a dramatic shot of her state championship run, her and Jet leaning hard into the last barrel, ready to explode into the straight run back to the gate.

"Someday, if you stick with it," she said. She glanced at her mother, who, in essence, had just volunteered her without even a consult. But she found she didn't mind, not with a kid who clearly loved horses this much. She'd find space in her schedule. Fortunately, her regular clients, the four-legged ones, didn't go by a clock for classes.

"All right then," Mom said briskly. "Jeremy and I need to get acquainted, so why don't you two"—she waved them off—"go on a ride yourselves."

It hadn't been a suggestion as much as an order to vacate, and Nic knew better than to resist. Besides, it suddenly occurred to her that she would like to see firsthand just how well he handled himself around a horse.

"You and my mother reached an agreement?" she asked as she headed back outside. He came along as if he'd recognized the command as clearly as she had.

"Yes. She's a powerhouse, and I think that's just what Jeremy needs."

He couldn't have said anything she liked more than that her mother was a powerhouse, because it was absolutely true.

"Shall we take that ride she suggested, then?"

He closed the door behind them, then turned to face her.

"Absolutely, Ms. Baylor."

She tilted her head as she looked at him. "Do you do that to annoy me?"

"What?"

"Call me Ms. Baylor."

His brows rose. "I call you Ms. Baylor because you haven't said I can call you anything else."

She suddenly remembered when she'd told Jeremy he could call her Nic. And the boy had, but not his father. She realized now that he hadn't interpreted the permission she'd given his son as permission for him to do the same. How very . . . old-fashioned of him.

It was a bit of a jolt for her to realize she liked that.

He held her gaze, and it was unsettling. She'd always thought they must use filters and such to get his eyes to look that startlingly blue, but now she knew better.

"My mistake," she finally managed to say. "Please, call me Nic."

"My pleasure," he said, and the way he said it sent a tiny frisson of just that through her.

Pleasure.

This was going to be . . . interesting.

Chapter Seventeen

"THAT'S QUITE A picture on the wall in there," Jackson said. He meant it. The dynamic, powerful duo of horse and rider practically burst out of the flat medium of the photograph, and when he'd first looked at it, he almost heard the echo of the roar of a Sunday rodeo crowd.

"It was a good year. Our best, in competition. That's why I retired on it."

"There's a lot of trust in that image."

She looked at him as if he'd startled her. Again. He didn't want to think how bad her initial opinion of him must have been if every normal thing he said surprised her.

"Yes. Jet and I had a strong bond. I rode him for most of my competitive career. He was a great horse, with a ton of drive and spirit."

Just like you, I suspect.

But he only said, "Was?"

A flash of sadness showed in her eyes for a moment. "Yes. We lost him last year. He was seventeen. He competed until he was twelve and still beat the younger horses."

"He sounds like one of a kind."

The sadness retreated, replaced by the glow of pride.

Pride in a beloved teammate. "He was. I never would have gone as far as I did without him. And that career and reputation he helped me build is the foundation of what I have now. I owe it all to him."

Jackson's throat tightened a little. For her to give credit to what some called a dumb animal told him a great deal about the character of this woman. But he had to admit, he liked her earlier apology even better. Because she couldn't have found a better way to say it.

. . . a kid like that couldn't have the kind of man I assumed you were as a father.

It seemed when Nicole—Nic, now that he had permission—Baylor apologized, she didn't mess around.

"Now," she said, snapping him out of the reverie, "let's find you a horse to ride."

He lifted a brow at her. "Got any bucking horses around?" She gave him a startled look. He shrugged. "Just wondered if you'd slide one in on me to see what happened."

"I wouldn't do that!"

He kept his expression even. "I think you might have a few days ago."

To his surprise, her cheeks pinkened. "I might have," she admitted. "But not now. And you," she added, her tone changing entirely as he let his grin creep through, "set me up for that."

"Yep."

For a split second, he wondered if he'd made her angry.

If he'd set them back to square one with his teasing. But then she burst into laughter, and his worry vanished, to be replaced by a warm, expanding feeling that made his grin widen.

Still smiling, she said, "You want a challenge, or a horse you don't have to worry about?"

Was this a test? "Depends. We taking a scenic tour?"

"I guess so," she said. Then, with a wry quirk of her mouth—he was starting to like that expression on her—she added, "It won't take nearly as long as it used to, since we're not the size we once were."

She said it as if a physical part of her had been removed. And he got the feeling that's how she thought of it, so attached was she to this land she clearly loved. Losing a big piece of it had clearly hurt.

And seeing her hurt stung him a little, which made him say almost hastily, "How about no worries now, and the challenge next time?"

"Done," she said, as if she was glad to move on quickly. And without, he noted, contesting that he'd be back.

They walked to a stall about halfway down on the right, and a dappled gray head popped out.

"Well, hi there," he said, as the horse looked at him with interest.

"This is Shade," Nic said.

It felt odd to him to even think of her that way, he'd been so careful about not using the nickname. And he felt a sudden qualm about that barrier having been removed. It had been a lot easier to ignore—or pretend to—those big eyes, that soft, kissable mouth, when that wall had been there. The wall of knowing she didn't like him had been an odd sort of protection. A protection he hadn't needed before, since no woman stirred him up anymore.

Until now.

The dark dapple gray nickered as if he'd recognized his name. He nudged at her until she rubbed his nose.

"Shade, this is Jackson," she said to the animal. "He's going to be yours for the day, so see to him, all right?"

The horse gave a whimsical-sounding snort, as if to say, *Like I ever do anything else?* Jackson couldn't help smiling.

In the next stall, another head turned to look, a black-and-white paint horse that looked a bit like Jeremy's favored pony in coloring.

"That'll be the challenge," Nic said when she saw him looking. "He's not mean, just spirited. Takes a stronger hand than the ranch sweetheart here."

She took the halter that hung on a hook outside the stall door and handed it to him. He took it, looked at her face, saw her very neutral expression.

"And so the testing begins," he said. He saw the flicker in her gaze and added quickly, "Which is as it should be. You need to know, for the sake of the horse, if I have a clue."

"Indeed," she said, and he thought he heard a note of approval in her voice. That low, sweet voice he was really trying to deny had an odd effect on him.

He spent a couple of minutes talking to Shade until the horse nudged him, much as he had Nic. Only then did he slip on and buckle the halter, then open the bottom half of the stall door. The gray stepped out the moment he turned around, no pull on the lead rope required.

They followed Nic to the other end of the barn and the tack room. A glance inside told him there were a lot of saddles racked up. "The brown King is his usual," she said, pointing to a well-used, but also well-maintained, saddle whose brand name happened to match one of his own. "But I don't know if it'll fit you."

Her gaze had shifted to his belt and below. He knew she was just assessing how he'd fit in the seat of the saddle, but it was still a bit disconcerting. He looked away as he said, "Better it not fit me than him."

"Good answer," she said, and when he glanced at her, she was smiling again.

He'd expected her to watch his every move while he tacked up the gray, but she didn't. She turned and walked back down the rows of stalls. Nevertheless, he went through his usual routine, given the horse's back a brushing to be sure all the hairs were going the right direction, then lifting the saddle pad aboard and sliding it back before going for the saddle. He checked the stirrup length, knowing by experience it was too short for him; being six foot one had its drawbacks. But he got enough by dropping the length to the max, then hooked the right one over the saddle horn to keep it from essentially kicking the gray in the ribs on the off side when he swung it over.

He knew Nic was back, he'd heard the *clip-clop* of the hooves of the horse she led. But he'd have known, anyway, because he could practically feel her gaze. Still, he didn't turn until he'd tightened the cinch just enough to hold the saddle in place for the moment, then went to get the bridle hanging on the same rack he'd taken the saddle from. He glanced at the bit, then at Nic. "Plain snaffle?"

She nodded. "Told you he's a sweetheart."

He smiled. "Lucky me."

He looked at the horse she'd gone to get, and it didn't surprise him that it was the same solid, muscular sorrel who looked as if he knew a thing or three. He liked the way the horse's reddish coat was set off with a mane and tail that almost matched her sandy-blonde hair. Together, they made a striking pair.

"Problem?" she asked, and he realized he'd been staring.

"No," he said quickly. "He just looks like Sorry, minus the blond mane and tail." At her look he explained, "He's the horse I rode the first season of *Stonewall*. He's a sorrel, and the nickname just stuck."

"Only the first season?"

Was she was thinking the horse had proved too much for him? For a guy whose business usually involved being assessed and judged, usually in a string of auditions, he wondered where this newfound sensitivity about it had come from.

"Turned out he was a little too spooky for the work. The noise and equipment set him off, and one day, while just waiting to start a scene, he got spooked, broke the tie line, and took off. Ended up in a mess."

He thought he saw realization flash in her eyes. "The mud flat."

So she knew. Maybe she'd even seen the video somebody had posted that had become a big deal, although he didn't see why. Anybody who loved horses would have done the same.

"Yeah. That one."

"Was he okay?"

He nodded. "Nothing that wouldn't heal. But they didn't have the time to wait for that, so they switched me over to Buck, and I've ridden him since. He's a good horse, and we've really bonded, but I still felt . . . a connection to Sorry."

"What happened to him?"

He grimaced. "They were going to get rid of him, and nobody would tell me to who or where."

She went very still, and he saw that she knew as well as anyone that that was not a good sign. And when she repeated her question, her tone was grim. "What happened to him?"

He couldn't stop the slight smile that went with his one-shouldered shrug. "I bought him."

Chapter Eighteen

O F ALL THE things she might have expected, that wasn't one of them. Nic hoped she wasn't gaping at him, but she wasn't sure she wasn't.

"You bought him?"

He nodded. Then, with a wry smile, he said, "They thought I was crazy. It was the first season, we didn't even know if there'd be another at that point, and it wasn't like I was rolling in money at that stage."

So he'd spent money he at that time couldn't spare, to save a horse he'd apparently bonded with. And now that he was likely raking it in, he'd walked away for the sake of his son. Yes, she had most definitely misjudged the man.

"What did you do with him?" she asked, genuinely curious.

"He's boarded at a rescue place at the moment. Someone my friend Tucker knows runs it. I pay them, and that helps them keep the rescue going."

Somehow she knew he was paying more than what a standard boarding fee would be. And that she was certain of this told her just how much her opinion of the man had shifted.

As they headed out, she had to admit he could ride. She could always tell when a rider was new or nervous. They were very aware of what they were doing. There was a certain tenseness in the way they sat, the way they moved. Jackson showed none of that. He was relaxed, with an easy posture and perfect minimal tension on the reins. Beyond the occasional pat of approval he gave Shade, which she herself often did when riding a new-to-her horse, she would have thought he and the gray were old friends.

Maybe it was that that made her decide to head out to her favorite spot on the ranch. She didn't take everyone there. Her mother joked that she hoarded it for herself, and perhaps she did. When they'd been in negotiations to sell off that big chunk of land, once she'd resigned herself to the necessity, her only demand had been that this spot stay theirs. And her father had stuck to his guns on that point, declaring it nonnegotiable from the get-go.

As they rode, she noticed he had the look of someone soaking things in. He didn't just look around, he studied. And, she guessed, absorbed. She had the odd thought that perhaps he was analyzing how the terrain they were portraying on *Stonewall* was so very different from the terrain they were crossing now. Which made her glad she'd decided to bring him here.

They headed up the slow rise, and she found herself mentally timing their progress, because she wanted to be sure she was watching him when they reached the top. She wasn't sure why it was important to her, but it was.

They crested the slope, and he immediately—and gently—reined in Shade. He stared out over the vista before them, the long, rolling undulation of the hills, with the glint of the Pedernales River in the distance. She saw his lips part and his chest rise as he took in a deep breath, as if the air were scented with some sweet scent he couldn't name.

"Whoa," he whispered, so low she wouldn't have caught it if she hadn't been looking at him.

He stared out at the hills, as if he'd never seen anything like this before. And Nic realized that, if this had been a test, he'd passed with flying colors. And perhaps it had been a test, a very personal one for her, because how someone reacted to this, her favorite place, meant a lot to her.

And told her a lot.

"In spring that's covered with bluebonnets as far as you can see," she said quietly. "And if you time it just right, at sunrise, they're the same color as the sky, and it's like you're in some endless tunnel of blue. There's a video on the Bluebonnet Festival website one of our local guys did with a drone at the exact right moment, and it's amazing."

He looked at her then. "You love this place. And I don't mean just this particular spot. You love this land."

"I do."

"I always had a . . . different sort of feeling when I came to Texas, that there's a . . . spirit about the place."

She liked the way he'd put that. "There is. And if it speaks to you, you'll never want to leave."

He looked back out over the hills. "I've never felt that way about a place."

"I'd say any spirit that was once there has been pretty well stomped out of California."

His gaze shot back to her face, and he gave her a wry smile. "I could not and would not argue that. Except to add that if you let it, it'll suck your own spirit right out of you."

She had never expected him to be so . . . aware. Somehow she'd always thought of people in his business as feeding on the kind of energy the place held, a kind of energy that might be powerful, but was fueled by actions and decisions she didn't much care for.

"Do you think maybe that's part of what happened with Jeremy?"

He nodded. "That's one reason I wanted him out of there. So after he said he wished the ranch on the show was real . . ."

Was that what had started this? A simple wish for the impossible, that had made this man come as close as he could to making that wish a reality? And never mind what it cost him personally?

"But . . . there have to be contracts, right?"

He shrugged. "They could nail me for that," he agreed. "At this point, to see Jeremy like he's been since we came here, I don't care."

It was real. He really was this man, not some lightweight pretender. And for some reason that made her a little giddy. "There's the start of a good, long, straight run just down this rise a bit. Want to give it a try?"

Those famous eyes brightened. He lifted the reins slightly and Shade's head came up. "Maybe you should ask him."

"Oh, he's always ready," she said with a grin.

She spun Sass around on his hind legs and started down the narrow track. When they reached the bottom, the wider trail rolled out in front of them.

"Now?" Jackson asked as Shade danced beneath him, knowing what was coming. He sat it easily, calmly.

"Now," she agreed, and put her heels to the eager horse.

"YOU KNOW, YOU could teach Jeremy to ride yourself."

Jackson paused in his brush down of Shade after the ride that had taken them twice as long as he'd expected, because she'd shown him most of the ranch. He knew she was unhappy that it was smaller than it had once been, but he laughed inwardly when he thought of the suburbs of L.A., where people bought a house on a couple of acres and called it a ranch. The romance of the lifestyle—or at least a pretense at it—was powerful even now, and even in places it was unsuited for.

He looked at Nic over the back of the gray. "No, I

couldn't."

"You could," she insisted. "You ride more than well enough. Better than I expected."

"I get the feeling you didn't expect much."

"True," she admitted, but with that flicker of a grin that made him feel . . . he wasn't sure what to call the little jolt it gave him. "But it's obvious now that I've seen you ride that you're more than adequate. A lot more."

"I think I'll have that etched on a plaque for my desk. 'More than adequate.'" He made sure he was grinning back at her when he said it.

She arched a brow at him, exaggeratedly. "You have a desk?"

He laughed, and the moment he did, so did she. He had to give her that much—when she changed her mind, she did it thoroughly. What would have been a genuine jab just a couple of days ago was now obviously a joke. This was the kind of lighthearted repartee he'd never thought to have with her.

Face it, you never thought you'd have it again with any woman, unless it was scripted for you both.

It was true he'd done scenes of this kind of teasing back and forth, sometimes with an actress who helped make it feel almost real, and sometimes with someone who made it a chore. But not since Leah had it come . . . naturally. Not from lines written on a page by someone else, but out of his own mind.

Maybe he was just relieved she wasn't jabbing at him and meaning it anymore. It would be hard to bring Jeremy here every day and put up with that. Of course, he could just drop him off, but he didn't want him out of his sight for that long just yet.

It occurred to him to wonder what he was going to do if this worked out. What was he going to do while Jeremy was with Mrs. Baylor? Not like he could expect Nic to go riding with him every day. She'd already arranged her schedule— she was quite in demand as a trainer, and obviously more than worth what he'd be paying her—so that she could teach Jeremy. But the appeal of even the thought of spending long rides with her startled him, and he had to rein it in harder than he had to rein Shade in all afternoon.

He'd been so focused on Jeremy, and once he'd seen how the boy seemed to blossom here, been determined to stay as long as necessary, that he hadn't really thought much about what he himself was going to do here. He needed to think about that. He thought about how fascinated Jeremy had been by the statue at the library and by the saloon building. Maybe he should spend some time scouting out other places like that, with historical significance.

Wouldn't hurt you to learn a bit either.

He'd thought he'd done that when he'd come to Texas twice before to get the feel for the show. But he'd been more focused on the people—how they acted, what their interests were—to try to bring life to the character of Austin Holt.

But now, here in this small town, he was feeling the pull of the land itself, and the incredible things that had happened in this state that had once been a country of its own.

So he would learn. Not for the role or the show, but because now he wanted to. And he had a sneaking suspicion it wasn't only for Jeremy's sake.

Chapter Nineteen

J ACKSON WAS HAVING trouble deciding, as he walked down the main street of Last Stand, if people were looking at him because they knew who he was or simply because he was a stranger in their little town. Back in L.A.—funny, it had only been a week, but already he wasn't thinking of it as "back home" anymore—he'd know, because they'd be all over him. Here, they looked, most even smiled, but nobody bothered him.

There was, of course, another possibility. That the Last Stand grapevine was not only efficient, but . . . kind. That seemed almost impossible to him, but then it had been the wife of the police chief who'd said she'd put the word out. Perhaps her word was law, as he suspected her husband's was around here. After all, not every small town had a bona fide national hero working for them.

A real hero. Not an actor playing a heroic part, but the real deal. Maybe that's why they left him alone. They knew the difference.

He kept walking, his cup of coffee from Java Time— which he found he liked better than the big chain stuff—

offering a welcome warmth on this chilly morning. He'd made himself leave after dropping Jeremy off with Mrs. Baylor for his day's lessons, to be followed by his reward of riding lessons on Pie with Nic. He was doing so well that after the first couple of days, Mrs. Baylor had said he should quit hovering. So he fought the urge to stick around and just watch the running of the ranch, the way real cowboys worked—and the way one particular cowgirl worked.

So instead he'd set out to learn this place where they'd landed. He'd been walking the side streets today. The ones that paralleled Hickory, where Tris's duplex was, were all tree names. The cross streets that paralleled Main Street seemed to be mostly flower names, including the somewhat whimsically named Yellow Rose Road. He'd always known Texans were proud of their home state, he'd just never quite realized how deep it went.

He was passing the hardware store—named *Nailed It*, which made him smile—when the door opened and a boy careened into him. He managed not to spill the hot coffee on him, but barely.

"Sorry, mister," the boy said quickly, nearly dropping the bag from the store. Jackson grabbed it with his free hand and kept it from hitting the sidewalk, which could have been a mess because he saw then it was full of nails and fasteners and other bits of hardware.

"Hey, you're that guy! The *Stonewall* guy."

The boy looked fourteen or so, maybe a little older. Not

exactly the audience they aimed at, but the show had gotten so huge, who knew where the audience pool ended anymore?

"Sorry," the boy repeated. "I know we're not supposed to bother you."

"You didn't," Jackson assured him. He looked at the bag. "Building something?"

"Yeah," the kid said eagerly, looking up at him with a pair of big brown eyes. "A house for my new dog. He's out in the truck. Keller—he's pretty much my dad—is going to help me."

Pretty much my dad?

"Lucas?"

The call came from inside, and the boy turned quickly. "Right here."

The man who stepped outside the store then looked like his horse should be tied up out front. Head to toe, all six-plus feet of him—the man had about an inch on him, Jackson guessed—was powerful, muscled cowboy. From the well-used boots up to the black felt cowboy hat. A pair of dark-green eyes looked at him assessingly, then flicked to the boy standing there.

"Going to introduce us?" the man asked.

"Oh, sorry," the boy said, like a kid suddenly reminded of manners he'd been taught. "This is Keller Rafferty, and I'm Lucas Brock." Which probably explained the "pretty much my dad" part. Adopted? Stepdad? Whatever, it was clear they had a good relationship, because the boy smiled up at him happily. "And you already know who this is, since Sydney loves the show. She's gonna be jealous we met you."

"Sydney's my wife," the man explained. "And his cousin," he added, nodding at the boy. At Jackson's expression, he grinned. "It's complicated, as they say."

"But good," the boy added.

"Yeah, it is," Rafferty said, reaching out to ruffle the boy's already tousled hair. Then he looked back at Jackson. "Welcome to Last Stand."

"It's quite a place."

"It's a good place."

"I'm getting that feeling. Lots of history here."

The other man chuckled. "You want that, you need my mom. She's a walking encyclopedia of Last Stand history. And she can tell it in a way that makes it come alive."

"You should come meet her," Lucas said eagerly. "Mrs. R is great."

"It's really my son who's interested."

Lucas started to speak again, then stopped. He glanced at Rafferty, who nodded. Then the boy started again. "She told me your son's mom was killed in a car crash."

Jackson tensed a little, although he told himself it was hardly surprising they all knew. But the boy's next words shocked him.

"So were my mom and dad. It was awful. Still is, sometimes." He hesitated again, then said, "Mrs. R said maybe, if I ever met him, I could talk to him about it. How it never goes away, but it does get better. She knows, because her husband was KIA. Keller's dad, I mean."

Jackson's gaze shot to the man standing beside this rather amazing kid. So his parents were dead, this man had lost his father, was married to the boy's cousin, and Lucas apparently lived with them. It made sense now. A joining of people who understood loss.

"It's up to you," Rafferty said quietly. "But if you ever think it would help, the offer's there."

"Thank you," he said. "It just might."

"Bring him out to the ranch," Lucas said. "He could meet my dog, and Mrs. R's. And Chance's dogs too. He rehabs military dogs."

Jackson liked that fact that the boy felt confident enough in his new, tragically altered life to make the invitation, knowing Keller Rafferty would have his back.

And as he watched them go, he acknowledged that he was a bit uncomfortable with this aspect of his life being a topic of discussion with strangers, but he knew it came with the territory. And he had the feeling these wouldn't be bad strangers to let in the door. Especially if they were going to be here awhile.

Between this family and the Highwaters, he was finding a lot of people to like here in Last Stand. Maybe this hadn't just been the best idea for Jeremy, but for him too.

When he arrived back at the Baylor ranch, Jeremy was, as he'd expected, happily aboard Pie in the main corral. What he hadn't expected was that he was still with Mrs. Baylor, only she was astride a compact, muscular bay right there in the corral with him. Nic was leaning on the fence, watching. Smiling. Widely.

He hesitated, afraid his arrival might put an end to that smile. He reminded himself they'd made peace, and she'd made that lovely apology, yet still he hesitated, not really sure why.

"Going to just stand there, or come watch?"

She hadn't even looked, yet she knew it was him? He found himself thinking he'd like to read something into that, then laughed inwardly at himself. This was the time they'd agreed on for him to pick Jeremy up, so why should he be surprised she knew it was him without looking? He walked over to the fence.

The moment he got there, three things happened fast. Jeremy spotted him and waved. Pie sidestepped a little, making the boy wobble a little and say "Whoa" in a way that had little to do with the classic horse command. And Jackson tensed, ready to go over that fence if the pony didn't settle. But he did, quickly, although he came to a halt as if confused.

Mrs. Baylor, ever the teacher, even here it seemed, calmly spoke to his son. "What do you think happened there, Jeremy?"

"I think I pulled on the reins when I waved to Dad," he said. "But I was still telling him to go forward, and he got confuzzled."

Jackson sucked in a breath at hearing the once familiar, joking combination of confused and puzzled that Leah had often used. He was sure the echo of that old pain was showing in his face, so he lowered his gaze to his hands where they rested on the top railing. He was aware the two riders had begun again, but couldn't look up just yet.

"It's okay. He's fine," Nic said.

"I know," he said without looking up. "It's just . . . his mother used to use that word a lot."

"It's a great word, on three levels. The definition of each, and then the combination that illustrates the very thing it's describing." He raised his head and looked at her, a little startled. She smiled rather impishly. "What can I say? I'm the daughter of a teacher."

He smiled back at her. "And a great teacher. I've never heard Jeremy so excited about what he's learning, even after only three days."

"She's the best," Nic said simply. Then, with another of those smiles, added, "Well, her and Mrs. Valencia."

"Second time I've heard that name come up. She must be something."

"She was one of those teachers who was legendary." She gave him a rather pointed look. "She retired to help her daughter look after her grandson, after his father was killed in action overseas."

He couldn't miss the point she was making, but he

didn't think it fit. Again, that was something actually heroic, not a safely conducted representation of it. Or maybe that was her point.

"Of course, now her daughter's married to a police detective, Sean Highwater. I guess some people are just attracted to . . . some people."

She looked away hastily, and he wondered why. But then Mrs. Baylor and Jeremy were heading for the gate, the riding lesson apparently over for the day. Jeremy was chattering, actually chattering, and Jackson didn't think he'd ever tire of hearing that enjoyment in his son's voice.

And that as much as anything decided him.

"As soon as you get him taken care of," he said, nodding at the flashy pony, "I need your help."

Jeremy blinked. "My help?"

"Yeah. We need to give your aunt her office back, so I thought we'd start looking for a place of our own."

His son's eyes widened, so full of hope Jackson thought his heart might have missed a beat. "Here? In Last Stand?"

"That sound good to you?"

Jeremy nodded so fiercely Jackson wanted to hug him. But he knew that would embarrass the boy in front of his teacher—his two teachers—so he didn't.

But it was a close thing.

Chapter Twenty

*D*ON'T DO IT. *Don't do it.*

It became a chant in Nic's head as they walked beside the horse and the pony and their riders back to the barn. It would be a simple, easy solution, but the very idea of it made her too edgy to even think about it seriously.

And the fact that her mother had given her that well-known questioning look the moment she'd heard Jackson say "a place of our own" told her she had thought of it too.

They stopped at the platform Dad had built. Mom ground-tied the patient horse, who was very used to this by now, and Nic went up on the platform to help. Her mother had this pretty well down, but it never hurt to be on standby, just in case.

Once she was back in her wheelchair, she headed down the long ramp, letting the chair pick up a little speed about halfway down, when it would be safe. She let out a whoop Nic knew was for Jeremy's sake, and the boy laughed.

"That's pretty cool," he said.

"Nobody wants to end up in a chair, but if you do, you grab your fun where you can," Mom said. "Did you know there's a famous barrel racer who got hurt like I did and still races? They even made a movie about her."

Jeremy's eyes widened. "Really?"

The boy glanced at his father, who smiled. "We'll find it and watch it," he promised.

"Now," Mrs. Baylor said, "Nicky has something she'd like to show you that might suit your needs."

"Mom!" She almost yelped it, making Jackson look at her curiously.

Her mother lifted an arched brow at her. "It would be the perfect solution, would it not?"

It probably would. And she'd have to come up with a pretty good reason not to even offer it, and the only one she could give her mother would cost too much in embarrassment. She couldn't even plead it wasn't fit to be shown, because she had just been there and tidied up.

"Dare I ask?" Jackson said, rather dryly. And he asked it of her mother, she noticed, no doubt having seen her own reaction.

"Nicky can explain," she said cheerfully. "Right now, I need to get inside for a video meeting."

Defeated, Nic watched her mother head for the house.

"She's busier than most agents I know," Jackson said.

She glanced at him, and he was smiling as he watched her mother go. Damn, he was hard to resist when he smiled like that, so warm and genuine.

"What's goin' on?" Jeremy asked.

"I'm not really sure," Jackson answered, then looked at

Nic directly, with those famous blue eyes. "What is going on?"

She sucked in a deep breath and let it out slowly, calmingly. "I guess I'm showing you something. So unless you feel like walking a half a mile or so, you might as well saddle up Shade. Jeremy, you can just stay aboard Pie."

"Cool," the boy exclaimed. Clearly, anything that involved more time in the saddle was good with him.

It took them twice as long to get there as it had taken her the other day, because they went slowly on purpose, so Jeremy and the pony could keep up. Jackson didn't seem inclined to chat idly, but then, he never did. He rode with the same ease she'd seen before and looked around with interest as they went. There were several of Dad's herd in the biggest pasture, and Jeremy spotted them immediately.

"I thought cows were brown," he said.

Before she could answer, his father did. "Those are special. Black Angus, they're called."

So did he actually recognize them, or had he been talking to Dad?

"Who's Angus?" Jeremy asked.

Jackson blinked, and Nic couldn't help chuckling. "Not who, where," she said. "Angus is a county in Scotland, where the breed originated."

"Oh," the boy said with a small nod, apparently satisfied.

"We could cut across the big pasture and get there in half the time, but Dad would have a fit if we disturbed his babies," she said. "And I'm only half joking."

"Get where? Or should I not ask?" Jackson said.

They were starting up the slight rise now, close enough that she might as well explain. "Our longtime foreman retired a while ago. He was ready, anyway, and after we sold so much acreage, we didn't really need a full-time guy, so we didn't hire a replacement. Which left his house empty."

Jackson's gaze sharpened, and she knew he'd gotten there. But Jeremy merely looked curious again, so she kept going.

"We've thought about renting it out, but since it's on the ranch itself, finding someone we could trust seemed daunting, so we've put it off."

They could see the building through the trees now, the small grove of live oak and pecan trees that had been Clark's favorite part of the location. They not only provided a bit of shade from the Texas heat, but they framed the view she herself loved. From the main house, all you could see was work. Barns, corrals, the driveway, all the things that needed maintenance. From here, on this slight rise, you could look out over the Hill Country she so loved without having the undone chores hammering at you.

She pulled to a halt in front of the expansive front porch that ran the width of the house. "It looks a bit rustic, because it was partially built out of the trees that were cleared to do it."

"Seems fitting," Jackson said. He'd said nothing about

the obvious reason they were here, which she knew he'd tumbled to the minute she'd mentioned the house was empty.

"We thought so. But it's up-to-date inside. Even has internet. Which is good because the cell reception is kind of lousy."

"Not sure that's not good too," Jackson said, and she looked at him just in time to see his eyes roll.

"It's cool," Jeremy decided, that apparently being his descriptor of the day. "Can we go look?"

"Tie up right there," she said, gesturing toward the old-fashioned hitching post to the right of the porch steps, "and have at it. I'll be right there to unlock the door."

The boy slid off Pie and did so, with great care, she noticed. Then he raced up the five steps to the porch, which was high enough to give an even better view.

She and Jackson followed at a slower pace. He was looking around intently, at the outbuilding that was both stall and feed storage, and the small corral next to it. There was a carport to one side of the main building, sheltered on three sides, and she saw that register too.

"No garage," she said. "Clark didn't need one, since he rode everywhere here, and borrowed one of the ranch trucks if he needed a vehicle."

He only nodded. Then they were up the steps, just as Jeremy exclaimed, "Wow, it's like you can see forever!"

He was leaning on the porch railing, looking out over the

view she loved. "It is," she agreed. "This is my other favorite spot on the ranch." She glanced at Jackson, who was staring out across the hills as intently as his son was. "Only thing missing is that glimpse of the river."

"It's still amazing," he said, still looking, scanning, as if he couldn't get enough of the view. It let her study his profile, and a beautiful profile it was. She'd never denied how good-looking he was, only that he didn't have a clue about the reality he was supposedly trying to portray. But she'd been wrong. About that, and other things as well.

"I can see how a man would get up in the morning, walk out here, maybe with a cup of coffee, and just . . . breathe it in. Look out over all this and be proud to be a part of it, part of what keeps it going."

He'd said it all quietly, as if to himself. As if he was just speaking his train of thought. He wasn't trying to flatter her or impress her. He didn't even look to see if she'd heard him.

Because he means it.

"Clark, our old foreman, used to say we put our house in the wrong place, where all you can see is the work to be done."

He did look at her then. "Maybe he was right. Because from here you can see why you do it."

Nic had no words to describe how that simple observation moved her.

"Yes," she said, past the tightness in her throat. "Our place is more convenient to the work, but this is where I would have put the main house, even if it did take a quarter of an hour to saddle up and get to work."

"I'd think it'd be worth the ride down. Give you time to think, to organize the day ahead."

"Exactly." She wanted to say something, to say out loud how much she agreed with him, and how it made her feel that he saw all this. But she was afraid of what might come tumbling out, so instead she walked over to where a small birdhouse hung from a branch of the oak tree that shaded that end of the porch. She reached underneath and opened a tiny drawer that was almost invisible from the outside to pull out the front door key.

"Hey! That's sneaky!" Jeremy exclaimed.

"Isn't it?" She grinned at the boy. "My dad built it." She lowered her voice to a conspiratorial whisper. "And now you know the secret, but you can't tell anyone."

"Promise," Jeremy said, making a cross motion on his chest and looking so pleased to be trusted it tightened her throat all over again. These Thorpe males were really getting to her.

She unlocked the front door and let Jeremy go in first. "It's all wood in here, too!" He seemed excited by the idea. The second thing he seemed to notice was the ladder leading up to the sleeping loft that overlooked the great room. To the right was a large stone fireplace, flanked by bookcases and a log rack that were empty at the moment. At the other end of the main space was a simple, but well-equipped Lshaped kitchen, with a small table and four chairs against the wall next to the short end of the L.

Jeremy had waited as long as he could, she suspected, before running over to the ladder. "What's up there?"

"Why don't you go up and see?" It was a stepladder-type structure with solid railings, so he should be fine, but she realized belatedly she probably should have checked with Jackson first. But it turned out it didn't matter, because Jeremy did just that.

"Dad?"

"Go ahead," his father said. "Just take it slow."

Her idea of slow and the boy's idea were a bit different, but he made it safely and, apparently, easily. He was out of sight the moment he hit the top, but his shout was clear. "Hey! There's a bed up here! And drawers, and a little table by a window where I can see the barn where Pie lives!"

When she glanced at Jackson again, he was shaking his head slowly, wonderingly. "I haven't heard this much energy from him . . . ever."

"Let me show you the rest," she said.

She led him down the hallway from the great room. The bathroom was on the left, and she pushed the door open. "There's only the one, but it's a nice size. Clark had that whirlpool tub put in. Said it was a luxury after a long, hard day."

There was also a sizeable shower, plenty of counter space, and a separate small room for the toilet.

"Nice," he said.

She tried to tell herself she was just showing the space, and the fact that the bedroom was next meant nothing in particular. She opened the door and stepped back to let him take a look. He stopped about five feet into the room and made a slow turn, checking it out.

She was glad to know everything was still tidied up after her visit last weekend. The room was big enough to hold the king-sized bed easily, and the dresser with its mirror was a suitable size, and all that was needed besides the big walk-in closet. And on the back wall was a desk that faced a large window with the downstairs version of the view Jeremy had crowed about up in the loft.

"Also nice," he murmured.

"Not too rustic feeling?"

"Wonderfully uncitified," he answered.

She loved the way he'd put it. And knew in that moment what his answer would be to the question she hadn't yet asked. She tried not to think about how this would complicate her life and focus only on how happy Jeremy seemed.

On the thought, the boy appeared, apparently wanting to see where they'd gone. "This is nice too," he pronounced.

Jackson turned around and crouched down to the boy's level. "You like it?"

"Yeah. That loft is cool. I'd like to sleep there."

He straightened up and faced her. "Is that what we're talking about here?"

"You need a place. It's empty," she said.

"Can I afford it?"

She blinked. Surely, money wasn't an issue, was it? She didn't know how much he got paid, but she was sure that by now, with the show a huge hit, it was a lot. He had to be a millionaire ten times over by now, at least.

"That you'd have to work out with my dad," she said, rather carefully.

"We're going to stay here? Live here, on the ranch?"

Jeremy sounded so excited Nic jettisoned all her doubts and worries. Crazy how she'd become so attached, so fast, but she would do a lot more than put up with a tenant in this house she loved for the joyous sound of that wounded boy's voice.

Chapter Twenty-One

JACKSON LEANED BACK in the chair and swung his feet up on the porch railing, thinking it felt both longer than ten days and shorter since they'd moved into this place. Tris had come along that weekend they'd moved what they had brought, and he had spent some time making calls to have some of their things shipped out from L.A. She put her stamp of approval on the place, although making clear they would have been welcome to stay with her however long they'd needed.

He'd told Jeremy to make him a list of what he wanted from home besides clothes, and when the boy had handed it to him it was short, and in a strange way, sweet. His photo of the three of them from the dresser, his roadrunner blanket, his five favorite books, his box of mementos—mostly reminders of his mother—and his Lego building kit. Jackson had more than once thought the boy was destined to be an architect because of the amazing things he put together with that box of plastic pieces. And he couldn't help thinking better that than a smartphone the boy had so far, thankfully, shown no interest in.

Then they'd done some local shopping, including another stop at the western wear shop for Jeremy. The boy had fallen in love with one of the carved leather belts on display, with intricate, detailed designs done by a local resident. Rylan Rafferty, the sign said. Jeremy had stopped to look, found one with a pinto horse on it that happened to be small enough for him, and that was enough.

"Rylan is just starting to experiment with colors on the belts, especially the kid-sized ones," the clerk, Nic's friend Hannah, had explained to the boy, giving him all the attention she would an adult, which Jackson liked. He'd smiled at her in thanks, which had apparently encouraged her.

"Still can't sell you a hat?" Hannah had asked, clearly teasing.

"Haven't earned it," he'd answered, and her surprised look changed to one of approval so quickly he knew he'd said the right thing. It registered with Nic as well, whose smile warmed him.

Nic, who had set aside her misgivings and brought them here, to this house, a perfect place with just enough privacy and yet with the new life Jeremy had plunged into enthusiastically close at hand.

Now he took a long sip of coffee as he looked out over the hills. He felt more relaxed, freer, than he had in a very long time. This was one of the best decisions he'd ever made. Maybe, after marrying Leah, the best.

He froze, holding the mug, staring out at the horizon, but not really seeing it. Because for the first time in three years, thinking of Leah hadn't brought that horrible jab of piercing, incapacitating pain. Oh, the ache was still there, the sadness, the melancholy, but it wasn't throttling. It didn't make his whole chest tighten until it was hard to breathe.

He'd watched Jeremy head out to go to his session with Mrs. Baylor this morning, with more eagerness than the boy had ever shown going to school. And after he reminded himself repeatedly they not only weren't in the city anymore, they were on completely private property, he'd let the boy go on his own, figuring the half-mile trek would eat up some seven-year-old energy and have him calmer by the time Mrs. Baylor settled in with him.

He had no doubt that going ahead with her had been the right decision too. Never had Jeremy come home from school so excited about what he'd learned that day. Not like he did now, almost every day eager to talk about it. And of course, his riding lesson on Pie.

For a while after Jeremy had gone, he'd had the distraction of watching part of the Angus herd being moved from one area to another, down at the bottom of the hill, but that hadn't lasted. And then he was back to thinking, facing the fact that he himself was about to go crazy.

Apparently, after three weeks, it was beginning to sink in back in L.A. that he'd really walked away. His phone was piling up messages from his agent, from Miles, from Swiff, the angry exec, and a dozen others, including a studio head who rarely bothered to reach out. The only calls he took were from Tucker, who kept him apprised.

"They're going nuts, buddy. Nobody really believed you meant it until the last few days. They thought they'd just give you the break and work around it until you came to your senses."

"I have come to my senses. Everything you ever told me about Texas was true. How'd you ever bring yourself to leave?"

Tucker had laughed. "The lure of Hollywood, and bigger money than a broken-down rodeo cowboy could make there."

"I'd think you could have done something big here, based on the name you built before you and that bull collided."

"Maybe. But I got tired of people looking at me with that pitying expression on their face. Besides, it worked out well for a friend of mine, who turned coming to Hollywood into gold for both of us."

"A friend who then abandoned it all," Jackson reminded him.

"For good reason," Tucker said, sticking by him as he always did. "Oh, by the way, the producers made a decision. They've put Austin on a plane that disappeared. Haven't shot the eps yet, but that's the plan right now. They're leaving the door open for you."

"If they saw Jeremy now, already so much better, they'd know I'm not going to be walking back through that door."

"I'm not sure they'd get it. Can't think of a one of them who would do the same, except maybe Miles, if he had a kid in trouble."

He'd come out here to sit and look out over the hills after that call too. Now he realized he'd already made it a habit when he needed to think. And at the moment all he could seem to think is that he had too much time to think. He was used to long days of getting ready to shoot scenes, shooting them, then reshooting them, reshooting them again, lather, rinse, repeat. While it wasn't all physical work, it was tiring, and without it, he was finding himself a lot more restless. Especially at night, when he had too much of that time to think and little to distract him.

He heard a sound off to his right, a rustle of branches—mostly bare this time of year—and then a tiny, but unmistakable, bawling sound. He set down the mug and got up, leaning over the railing and looking in that direction. It took him only a moment to find the source, a small black calf entangled in a fallen branch down the hill a few yards.

The little animal didn't seem frightened of him when he got there, so he must be used to human handling. At least that's what Jackson told himself as he worked to get the calf free. He'd probably wandered off from the cattle he'd seen being moved earlier, although how the little guy had ended up here, he had no idea. But he was obviously one of Mr.

Baylor's prized Angus.

Once he'd gotten the calf clear, he pondered just letting him go and hoping he found his way back to mom—who had to be going crazy—but then he noticed he had blood on his hand. A quick check showed a long scrape on the calf's far side, likely by the broken part of the branch that had entrapped him.

"Okay, little buddy, I think you need some personal attention."

Little, he discovered when he picked up the baby animal, was a relative term. He was small for a cow, but he still weighed a good one-twenty at least. Enough that Jackson didn't want to lug him all the way down to the ranch house. So instead he headed for the carport. He braced himself on the side of the car as he opened the hatch, then grabbed the packing blanket that was still there from the move of the things they'd had shipped. He spread it out, then put the injured calf down. He seemed to settle, although Jackson wouldn't be surprised if he ended up with a bit of a mess to clean up before this was over.

He had to run inside to grab the keys, but when he got back outside and looked, the calf was still lying on his side, albeit looking around curiously. He took a moment to pat the little guy before he got in and started the motor. He figured his best bet was to just go and worry about any escape attempt or damage done after the fact.

He went as fast as he thought he safely could, and since it

was barely over a half mile, it only took a couple of minutes to get down to the main barn where, thankfully, he saw Mr. Baylor. The man waved, then turned as if to keep going into the barn, but stopped when Jackson pulled up close to the barn and parked.

Moments later he'd explained and they had the calf, who was up on his hooves now, out of the vehicle. And the mess he'd been afraid of thankfully didn't happen until he was out and on the ground.

Mr. Baylor looked at the wound with the calm of long experience. "We'll get this cleaned up and keep them in a stall for a day or two, and he'll be fine."

"'Them' means with mom, I assume. I'm guessing he'll be hungry soon, if he isn't already."

Mr. Baylor nodded, then gave him an up-and-down look that seemed to be approving. And maybe a little bit surprised. And Jackson recognized the look; he'd seen it often enough in another pair of eyes that looked exactly like these.

"Thanks for rescuing the little rascal," the man said.

"No problem," Jackson said. Then, without any real forethought, he added, "I'd like to do more."

"You're already paying more rent than we'd ever expected to get out of that place," Nic's dad said with a grin.

Jackson couldn't help smiling back; those negotiations had been . . . interesting. Richard Baylor had actually turned down his first offer, not because it was too low, but because he said it was too high.

It doesn't matter to me that you can afford it, it'd still be gouging. I don't hold with that.

Having come from a place where he doubted he'd ever hear those words spoken, Jackson had been struck speechless. And they'd settled on splitting the difference, which Jackson had insisted was fair because he was throwing Jeremy into the mix, and who knows what a seven-year-old boy fascinated with everything about this place could get into. Plus, the man had promised everyone on the ranch would look out for Jeremy, which was worth more to Jackson than he could express. And despite what Nic might think about his occupation and how it happened, he was used to working, and working hard. The first few days were nice and relaxing, but not doing anything long term was starting to wear on him.

"I feel like I'm just killing time, waiting for Jeremy, when there's work to be done all around me," he said.

"Now that's an attitude I can admire," Mr. Baylor said. "You volunteering?"

Jackson felt suddenly self-conscious. What was he worth around here, on a real ranch? Horses, yes, he could handle them, but from what he'd seen, they were only part of the life and work here. But there had to be stuff he could do, as just another body if nothing else.

"I guess I am," he said. "I know I don't know much about the reality of this life, but there must be some grunt work I can do, freeing up somebody who does know what they're doing."

"Well, well," Nic's father said, smiling. "Let's just see what we can figure out."

Chapter Twenty-Two

"SO JACKSON THORPE is really working on your ranch?"

Nic was used to the question by now. And her answer, which once might have been snide or snarky, was honest and simple now.

"He is," she told the clerk at the feedstore as he brought up her special order of grain for Pie, who, with Jeremy, was getting a lot more exercise than he had in a while and needed more than just forage. "And he's working hard."

"So it isn't all fake?"

"Not his willingness to work. Dad says we should be paying him, or at least lowering his rent." She'd been surprised anew herself at the energy and effort he poured into it.

You'd think you'd be tired of being surprised by now. Why don't you just admit you've entirely misjudged the man from the beginning, and stop?

She pondered that as she loaded the big bag of feed into her truck. She wasn't usually so resistant to admitting the obvious. Jackson Thorpe was no Hollywood phony who didn't like getting his hands dirty. He was a loving, caring father who'd upended his entire life and quite possibly ruined a burgeoning career for the sake of his son and ended up working as hard as any hand—and harder than some they'd had—on the ranch.

And speaking of fathers, her own seemed to have developed an annoying habit of picking the man whenever she needed a bit of extra muscle on a task, or suggesting he go with her if she had to head out somewhere on the ranch.

"He appreciates it, Nicky. Both the ranch and the opportunity to ride when it's not in front of a camera."

Camera or not, he could ride. She couldn't deny there was something about a good-looking man who sat a horse the way he did that pleased her in a very visceral way. Not that there weren't a wealth of them around Last Stand. The police chief, for starters, the Rafferty brothers, and a few others she could name. Yet none of them set her off the way Jackson Thorpe did.

Jackson Thorpe, the man she would have least expected to react to, that way. She'd thought herself immune. And she would have been, if he'd been the kind of man she'd assumed he was.

"Hey, Baylor!"

She turned to see Gary Klausen, who worked at the hardware store. "Hi, Gary."

"Y'all get that sliding door fixed?"

She nodded. "Once we got the right part, thanks to you."

He chuckled. "Thank your famous ranch hand. He's the

one who found it. I didn't even realize we had it in the store. Y'know, he's a really nice guy. Not at all snobby, like I would have expected. He helped me stack some heavy boxes and even helped Mr. Mason carry out a big load of lumber and tie it down."

She supposed it was progress, that she was no longer surprised that Jackson had done that. Twice more she met people she knew in town who had had an encounter with "their famous new resident," as one called him. And no one had a bad word to say about him. There was nothing but praise . . . and shock that he was so down-to-earth, which reminded her rather painfully of her own misjudgment.

If Jackson Thorpe had set out to charm Last Stand, he couldn't be doing better. But she knew now, this was simply who he was.

She stopped by Java Time for a coffee for the drive back home, mentally planning dinner since it was her turn to cook. She was contemplating shelving all her ideas and stopping at Valencia's to pick up a meal, since she had to practically drive by it, when she realized she knew the woman in front of her in line who had just said hello.

Jackson's sister. She hadn't realized how late in the afternoon it was, but if she, a teacher, was here, school was obviously out. And a bit to her own surprise, she found herself suggesting they take one of the open tables and sit for a few minutes before venturing back out into the chill of a Texas January. Chill being relative, of course, she knew.

"I can't thank you enough," Tris said without preamble. "I haven't seen either my brother or Jeremy this . . . calm, this much at peace, since Leah died."

Nic didn't think she'd mistaken the shadow that flickered in the other woman's eyes. "You were close to her?"

"Very. She was the sister I never had."

"So it was just you and Jackson?"

Tris nodded. "It's funny. I'd hear my friends complain about their little brothers, what a pain they were, and how embarrassing. And I won't say there weren't moments, but for the most part, Jackson was my best friend growing up, even though he's two years younger. He's always been there for me."

Nic smiled, although as an only child, she didn't really know firsthand about that kind of sibling bond.

"I was a junior when he hit high school," Tris went on, "and by then, he'd already shot up to nearly six feet tall. There was this guy bothering me, and one day he cornered me, and I nearly didn't get away. Jackson saw the bruises and guessed what happened. The next day that guy showed up at school with a black eye and a split lip, and avoided me like the plague. Jackson never admitted it, but I knew. I almost felt sorry for the guy, the humiliation of getting clobbered by a freshman. Which was what kept Jackson out of trouble . . . the clown was too embarrassed to admit what had happened."

Nic grimaced. "I'm sorry you had to go through that, but

that was good of him."

Tris grinned then. "The best part was after that, Jackson insisted on teaching me how to fight. Just in case I ever had to again, I could get away myself. He told me, 'Fight dirty if you have to, because only a dirty guy would do that to a girl who said no.'"

Nic grinned back because she couldn't seem to help it.

She was still thinking about that encounter when she got home. She saw Jackson helping Dad shift some hay bales in the barn, and automatically assessed the number they had left. Plenty to get them through to spring and the next harvesting. Then the scramble would begin to move the remaining bales to the front for usage and stacking the new season's behind it. It took up a lot of barn space, but not losing a chunk of the supply from spoilage was more important.

For a moment she just stood there, watching her father and Jackson work together. Despite his heart attack, Dad was a tough, strong man used to ranch work, but Jackson seemed to be keeping up just fine. And, she had to admit, she liked watching them work together. She liked watching Jackson work, period.

Which is why you end up watching it at night, in your dreams, so often?

That chiding inner voice did nothing to slow the heat that rose in her, because those dreams she'd been having never seemed to end with just watching him. She'd always thought women who dreamed about celebrities a bit silly, and telling herself it was the real man, not the actor she was making up nighttime scenarios about, didn't help much.

When they'd shifted the last bale and Dad nodded in that way that told her the job was done, she started walking toward them. But before she could say anything more than hello, Jackson's phone rang.

"Hollywood calling?" Dad asked, his tone joking.

"Nope, they're all routed directly to voicemail," Jackson said cheerfully. "Only my sister and Tucker get through, and I just talked to Tris."

He'd just talked to Tris? Like just now, after she'd run into her at the coffee shop? She couldn't stop the stab of curiosity about what his sister might have said.

He'd turned slightly away, but she couldn't help hearing when his voice powered up a little. "They're what?" And a moment later, he said, almost fiercely, "No. No, I want him. I'll transfer the money, whatever it takes. Can you see if Rachel can take him at the rescue until I figure something out?" Another pause. "Thanks, T. Let me know."

For a moment after he ended the call, he just stood there, clearly thinking.

"Bad news?" her father asked, saving her from having to do it.

Jackson looked at Dad and grimaced. "They were going to rid of Buck. The horse I rode on the show."

"The buckskin?" Dad asked, startling her. How had he

known that? Had he been secretly watching, too, with Mom?

Jackson nodded. "He's a great horse."

"Then why get rid of him?" she asked, curiosity overcoming her reticence.

"Apparently, he's been acting up a little," Jackson said.

"No surprise," she retorted. "Whenever I see shows with horses, I always feel bad for them, constantly being burdened with riders who know nothing." That had come out a little too close to her old prejudices, so she quickly added, "Present company excepted."

He shrugged, but she thought she caught a tiny smile at her words. "We got along, Buck and I."

"One-man horse, eh?" Dad said, and he was smiling widely.

Jackson's mouth quirked at one corner in that way she'd come to like seeing. *Face it, you just like his mouth . . .*

"I guess," he said, looking both pleased and worried.

"So you're going to buy him too?" she asked.

"He'd probably be okay. He just needs a rider with more experience, but . . ."

"Probably isn't good enough," she said, staring at this man she'd so misjudged.

"No, it's not," he agreed.

"Assuming you're going to be staying awhile, you could bring him here," Dad said. Jackson looked startled. "Your other one too. You could keep them in the little barn up at your place."

Your place.

"You'd . . . be okay with that?" Jackson asked her father, sounding almost as startled as he'd looked.

"You wouldn't be the first ranch hand to bring their own horse," Dad said easily. "And son, you've been working like one."

And suddenly, in Nic's mind, the dreams she'd had about someday making that house on the hill hers collided with him already living there, and she was thinking of what it would be like if both those things came together.

She almost laughed out loud at herself, at the crazy way her brain had put that together.

She wasn't laughing at all at the way her heart responded to it.

Chapter Twenty-Three

"THANKS FOR THIS," Jackson said to the man beside him as they watched the two boys deep in conversation while brushing the tri-colored dog, who stood for the ministering patiently.

"Don't thank me," Keller Rafferty said. "Like Lucas said, it was my mother's idea, and he agreed immediately. He remembers how awful it was for him, and he was over twice Jeremy's age when his parents were killed."

Jackson watched Jeremy's expression, which alternated between brow-furrowed seriousness to smiling delight, when the Aussie-Border collie mix swiped a doggie kiss over his cheek.

On his other side, Nic laughed in almost equal delight. "I'm thinking he needs a dog to take care of."

Jackson looked at the woman who had driven them over to the Rafferty ranch, saying she hadn't had a chance to talk to Maggie Rafferty in a while. She was smiling so widely as she watched his son, anyone would have thought Jeremy was hers.

His breath jammed in his throat at his own thought. It

felt like a bit of a betrayal of Leah, liking it so much, but how could he not when she looked at his lost little boy that way?

You're the problem, not her.

"I agree," Maggie Rafferty said as she came up beside them, carrying a tray holding a half-dozen mugs of hot chocolate. "And it so happens Chance has a prime candidate. You'll have to come back and meet him, when Chance gets back."

Nic looked at the older woman with some surprise. "A dog that would work for a little boy?"

Maggie nodded. "This one's different. It's a golden retriever he took in from a friend, not because he made the list."

Jackson had known only what Lucas had said that day they'd first met, that Chance Rafferty was former military himself, but now rehabbed military dogs. It was Nic who had told them, on the way here, that his organization, *They Also Serve*, took on the dogs the military had given up on. The ones who made the euthanasia list.

"They'd be put down if he didn't take them. He brings them here and works nothing short of miracles with them. And any who simply can't be brought back to normal life, who are too traumatized—which for Chance has been exactly two the entire time he's been doing this—he keeps. They live out their days on the ranch."

When she'd smiled, it had been one of admiration. And

since it was a more than admirable cause, there was no reason for it to make him a little grumpy. After all, he greatly respected Chance, both for his service and for what he was doing now, so it made no sense.

Well, one thing would make it make sense, but he wasn't going anywhere near the crazy thought that he didn't like how much she clearly liked the guy.

"What does 'put down' mean?" Jeremy asked from the back seat.

Jackson winced, and Nic shot him an apologetic look. "Shouldn't have said that, sorry."

He understood. She wasn't used to having little ears that didn't miss anything around. And that she felt bad about it only made him like her more.

But Jeremy had asked, and he'd made a vow never to lie to his son, and so he told him the truth.

"They kill them?" The boy sounded horrified, and why not? So was he.

"Because some of them, after being at war, aren't safe around people. They can't tell enemy from friend, or everything's a threat in their mind."

"But they were only at war for us," Jeremy protested.

And that's when, as Nic had slowed the car, she had looked back over her shoulder at Jeremy and said, "And that's why you and Chance are going to get along great."

As a diversion, it was perfect. It didn't deny the brutal truth, but it gave Jeremy something else to look forward to.

He wanted to thank her for that, but her attention was back on the road as she made the turn toward the Rafferty ranch, and he didn't want Jeremy to hear him say it and ask why. So he had done the only thing he could think of. He'd reached out and covered her hand with his and squeezed slightly. She'd given him a startled look, and he'd mouthed, "Thank you."

He had no words for the feeling the smile he'd gotten then had given him. He'd been relieved when they stopped at the ranch house and Lucas and Keller had been there to welcome them, and he had been able to shove that unfamiliar emotion back into its box.

"—that's Chance, never let down a brother-in-arms," Maggie was saying when he tuned back in to the present with a jolt. "So Atlas became Tri, his handler's widow came to adopt him, and Chance fell in love with her, and she, him."

She was patiently holding the tray, which now held two last mugs, her own—judging by the painting on the side that was the image of the dog the two boys had brushed to a shine—and one he obviously should have already taken.

"Sorry," he muttered, picking up the mug. And for lack of anything else to say, he complimented her on her own. "Nice image. Looks just like your dog."

"Because it is," she said with a smile. "My son Rylan did it for me a few years ago."

"He's the one who does the belts they have in the store in

town?" Jackson asked.

"The very one," she answered proudly.

"Jeremy has one. He found one with a pinto like the pony he's been riding, and he practically begged for it." His mouth tightened a little. "He hasn't asked for anything since his mother was killed. Until we came here."

"Last Stand is a good place," Maggie Rafferty said. "It was built by good, brave people, and it draws those same kind even now." She gave him a rather intent look before adding, "Obviously."

He felt more complimented than he had when he'd won his first Emmy Award, or when *Stonewall* had topped the streaming charts for months on end.

"I hear you're taking on a lot of work over at the Baylors' place. That's good. Richard had a heart attack a while back, but he insists on trying to do everything he did before."

"I didn't know that," Jackson said. But he wasn't surprised Nic's father hadn't mentioned it. He wasn't the type to whine. Nor was the woman before him now. "How did you do it? When . . . your husband was KIA?"

She shrugged. "It had to be done. My husband loved his boys, so I had to make sure they turned out as he would have wanted. They have." She glanced at her eldest son, who was sitting at the table with the boys and Nic, sipping at the hot chocolate he hadn't even tasted yet. "But as much credit goes to Keller as to me. He was only seventeen when Kyle was killed, but he stepped up for me and his brothers. Gave up any other life he wanted to make sure they were seen to."

Jackson found himself pondering at length the differences between this place and the place he'd left behind. It wasn't just the topography or the climate, it was the difference in the people that stunned him the most. Not that he hadn't met good people in L.A., he had, but he'd met far more who either cared nothing about anyone but themselves or made caring gestures only for the positive press it might gain them.

Here, it appeared to be simply the way things were done.

Jeremy was very quiet when they got in the car to head back home. Back to the Baylor ranch, he mentally corrected, although home felt like a much more accurate word for it. He couldn't quite believe they'd been here nearly a month. It had flown by, and between watching his son emerge from the cocoon of his overwhelming grief and enjoying the work he'd taken on, he couldn't remember ever being more content. He'd been delighted when they'd given him the plum role of Austin Holt, jubilant when *Stonewall* had hit so big, and utterly blown away when he'd come home with that first gold statue.

But this quiet, deep contentment was something he'd never known before.

It wasn't until they were there—Nic had driven them up to the porch—that Jeremy spoke. And then it was to ask Nic if she was going to come in. She looked surprised, so Jackson quickly offered to put on coffee. And Jeremy offered to share his favorite new discovery, the peach crisp from the Kolaches bakery in town.

"Now, how could I resist that, since it's my favorite too?"

They were seated at the small table, Jeremy tackling his treat with a gusto he also hadn't seen in a while. The boy had put on some much-needed weight in the month they'd been here too. He loved sleeping up in the loft, and Jackson liked having him there so he could hear clearly when he was downstairs. It had taken a couple of weeks of listening before he dared believe that perhaps Jeremy truly was past the nightmares and crying himself to sleep. He remembered thinking that all the physical work he himself had been doing had produced some solid sleep at night for him, so maybe all the learning and playing with Pie was doing the same for Jeremy.

Jackson glanced over at the fireplace, where he'd thrown on a new log to ramp up the heat; the evening chill was growing fast. He'd never really thought about Texas having cold nights, but for him the predicted mid thirties tonight qualified. The house had a decent heating system, but Jeremy loved the idea of heating it with the fire. "Like the pioneers did," he'd said.

Yes, his boy had come a long way in a short time. Today had been proof of that.

"Thanks for driving us out there," Jackson said.

"I was glad to. Haven't seen Maggie in a while."

"She's quite something."

"She's a dynamo. They're one of the founding families, you know."

"The originals?" he asked, remembering what she'd called them.

"Exactly. The Raffertys were in the middle of the last stand."

Jeremy's head came up. "I saw their name in the book Joey showed me. They were there and fought and everything."

"Right alongside the Highwaters," Nic agreed with a smile.

"Wow." The boy went silent for a moment, then, not looking at either of them, he said very quietly, "Lucas's mom and dad died."

"I know," Jackson said, almost as quietly.

"They put him in a home for orphans. He hated it and ran away."

He hadn't known that. "How did he end up at the Raffertys?"

"He was hiding there, 'cuz people were looking for him to send him back. But Keller let him stay. An' now he's adopting him."

"Keller Rafferty is a good man," Jackson said.

Jeremy looked up then. "Lucas said he was as happy as he could be. But that I was lucky to still have you."

Jackson didn't know what to say to that. How many sleepless nights had he spent thinking he wasn't up to this, raising his son alone? How many times had he thought with utter certainty that Jeremy would have been better off if he'd been the one whose vehicle had been broadsided and sent flying by that stolen car?

"You are," Nic said softly. "You have a father who loves you more than anything."

And again, Jackson was at a loss for words. Which didn't really matter because he doubted he could get them out past the lump in his throat, anyway.

Jeremy took another couple of bites, then gave Jackson a sideways look. One he recognized. And the shift in tenor made him able to speak.

"Out with it," he said, smiling so the boy would know he was teasing him.

"Can we really go back and meet the other dog?"

"I think we can manage that," he said, and if he'd been undecided, the look of excitement in his son's eyes would have made the decision for him.

"But you said we couldn't have a dog back . . . there."

Back there. As if Jeremy also was already thinking of this as home, and L.A. as just that other place they'd lived.

"It wasn't practical there," he said. "Or fair to the dog, because it would be left alone so much."

"They're pack animals," Nic put in. "And they need to be with their pack."

"And their people are their pack," Jackson added.

"So . . . we could have a dog here?"

Jackson leaned back in his chair and grinned at the boy. "I think it's almost a requirement. Right, Nic?"

"Absolutely," she said solemnly. "In fact, we're a little short on canines around here these days."

Something he should have asked before he'd started this—why did being around her screw up his logic so badly?—hit him. "So are you saying it would be all right, having a dog around? No 'No Pets' policy on the rental agreement?"

"Well, since the rental agreement was you and Dad shaking hands, I'd say he's the one to ask. But I know what the answer will be."

Jeremy let out a whoop of excitement and turned his attention to gobbling down the last few bites of his dessert and gulping down his milk.

"Homework?" Jackson asked when he was done.

"Yeah. Going now," Jeremy said without protest, and headed up the ladder to the loft.

Nic watched him go, then turned back. She caught Jackson watching her, but she only smiled, to his relief.

"Mom says he's doing great," she said.

"He said she's different from any other teacher he's had. In his whole three years of going to school, anyway. He said she makes it interesting."

"It's easier when it's a really smart kid."

She took another sip of coffee, not complaining that it was plain, ordinary. He tried to think of a woman he'd dealt with back in L.A. who wouldn't wrinkle her nose at plain, black coffee. Even Leah had preferred at least a fancy sort of creamer in hers. The silence between them began to seem awkward, and he searched for something, anything, to say. Started to speak, but lost the thought when she smiled at him over the rim of the coffee mug.

So here he was, the big star—or at least former big star, he'd blown that to smithereens now—in his new home, with a beautiful woman, a woman who fascinated him, and he couldn't think of a single thing to say. Or do. Except, looking at her mouth as she smiled, wondering what it would be like to kiss her.

He thought he managed to conceal the jolt of heat that went through him at just the thought. Quashing the urge wasn't quite as easy. In the end, only one thing enabled him to do it—the realization that as easily as he could hear Jeremy up in the loft from here, Jeremy could hear down.

And he grimaced inwardly at the idea that the only thing keeping his suddenly reawakened libido in check was his seven-year-old son.

Chapter Twenty-Four

I DIDN'T TRIGGER *that, did I?*

Nic stared down into the remaining dark, strong coffee in her mug, but all she saw was a replay in her head of that moment when something bright and hot had flashed across Jackson Thorpe's face.

True, it was gone a moment later, but she was certain she'd seen it. Certain because it matched her own unexpected gut reaction to that moment when she'd realized he was watching her. Watching her with a kind of longing, almost hunger, in those famous, striking dark-blue eyes.

So, what, as soon as she admitted he wasn't what she'd thought he was, she threw open the gates? Given some sign, some unconscious signal that she would now welcome what she would have recoiled at before?

The realization that she wouldn't recoil at it now made her set down her coffee mug before the ripples in the dark liquid made it obvious how unsettled she was.

Scrambling for something, anything, to distract her suddenly rowdy mind, she said rather abruptly, "Mom said you've never played a bad guy."

"No. Confused, conflicted, could go bad if pushed, yes.

But an actual bad guy, no."

"Why?"

He shrugged. "I'd like to say I don't have it in me, but I think everybody has the potential. That's just not the portrayal I want to be linked to. Not the emotions I want to channel."

She tilted her head slightly, studying him. "Is that what it is to you? You channel emotions through the parts you play?"

"Sounds all touchy-feely, I know, but sort of, yeah. Somewhere in the back of my mind, I tell myself there are people out there feeling the same way this guy, this character does, and if I do it right, they'll know they're not alone."

Nic stared at him now. She had never thought of it that way, but it made sense that seeing a character who had become real to you suffer could actually make you relate to them even more.

"Mom said something like that, after she watched a scene where someone in the TV family died. She said she knew the minute she saw it that you'd been there."

She was almost sorry she'd said it when he winced a little.

"That was just a few months after Leah was killed. I didn't plan on . . . using that pain, putting it on public display. But I had to think about how the character would be feeling, and . . . it just sort of happened."

"That must have been harrowing."

He let out a compressed breath. "The minute the director on that one yelled cut, I walked off the set. Told him to get what he needed out of what he had, because I wasn't doing it again."

And she guessed from the finality in those last words that he was also through talking about it.

"I don't know how you did it the first time," she said quietly, and left it at that.

She took another sip of coffee and looked around, toward the big great room where the fire now crackled happily in the big stone fireplace.

"I always liked this house," she said, watching the flames, figuring he wouldn't mind the abrupt change of subject. Judging by the way his tone changed, he didn't.

"I can see why. It's the perfect combination of spacious, with the high ceilings, but homey, with the relatively small footprint, the rustic feel, but all the conveniences. And the location's unbeatable."

She'd glanced at him when he started to speak, but by the time he'd finished, she was practically gaping at him. He'd verbalized her exact thoughts about the house he now lived in.

The house she'd often thought she'd like to live in herself.

And again, the images slammed into her brain, of them doing just that, living together under this vaulted roof.

A noise broke the flood. It was the sound of Jeremy coming down the ladder. He came running toward them, something in his hand, and with a different kind of shock, it hit her that she was happy, happy in a way she'd never known before, to see the boy acting so . . . normally. He'd come a long way in the month they'd been here, and it did her heart a new and unfamiliar kind of good to see it. She felt so attached to the child, and not simply because she was teaching him to ride. She felt connected in a kind of way she'd never known before. He mattered to her, a great deal, and when the inevitable moments of sadness swept over him, she felt a physical pain herself.

"I almost forgot. Mrs. B said I should show you this," Jeremy said as he skidded to a stop beside the table, a sheet of paper in his hand.

Jackson took it, saying in a clearly teasing tone, "She makes you do stuff on paper instead of on a computer?"

Jeremy shrugged. "S'okay. I didn't have to write something long."

Jackson looked at the page in his hand. Nic could see it was a paragraph in rather wobbly printed letters that were still quite readable. The green-inked paragraph below it she knew was her mother's writing, both from the ink color— she always said that she didn't like using red on children's papers, she wanted the subtle signal to be go-ahead green, not stoplight red—and the flowing style of the cursive.

She glanced at Jackson's face as he read her mom's note. And she knew she hadn't mistaken the sudden sheen in his eyes. He blinked a couple of times, proving her right.

"Is it bad?" Jeremy asked anxiously, looking at his father. "I don't read that curvy writing so good."

"No, it's not bad." Jackson's voice held a husky note she found shiveringly emotional. "Not bad at all. It just reminded me of something we haven't done in a while."

"Oh. You mean when you'd read me stories at night? I told her that's how I knew about that book."

"Yes."

There was a moment of silence before Jeremy said, almost shyly, "I miss that."

"Me too," Jackson said, his voice still noticeably tight. "How about we start that again? Pick out a book and we'll do it tonight."

There was no mistaking the way Jeremy's face lit up. Without another word, he turned and ran across the great room to the ladder and scrambled up to the loft. He hadn't needed to speak. The delight on his face was reaction enough. And a glance at Jackson told her he hadn't missed it. She felt a new kind of emotion at the blatantly obvious love this man had for his son.

He sat, staring down at the paper in his hand for a long, silent moment, and she had the feeling he was trying to rein in his emotions.

"May I?" she asked, gesturing at the single page.

He didn't answer, but handed it to her without looking up. At the top, in childlike, but clear enough printing, was a paragraph describing his favorite book. She didn't recognize the title, but to her surprise, the summation of the story of two kids and a dog who find themselves in the middle of nowhere trying to get home was nearly perfect and had her curious about the book itself.

Her mother's familiar hand, in the green-for-go ink, said much the same thing, but ended with, *This is excellent, well above the expected for Jeremy's age. He told me how you often read stories to him at night, doing all the different voices. He misses that. Now that you have more time of your own, perhaps you could revisit the habit. It might help in other ways too.*

"Now there's something not every kid has. A father who can do all the parts reading stories to him." He looked at her then, and he was still blinking a little too fast. "And I'd bet it was fun for you too."

"It was. It is. I should never have let it slip by the wayside."

"Hard to do when your world's been turned upside down. Sage Highwater told me that after their father was killed, just getting up in the morning seemed like too much."

"Sage?"

"Youngest Highwater, and the only girl." She smiled. "Another case of the oldest brother stepping up. Their flaky mother was long gone by then, and Shane gave up some big dreams to come home and see to his siblings."

Something different came into his voice then, something warmer and less rattled. "Seems you grow them that way here in Texas."

"We do," she said, and she didn't try to hide her pride in her home state. Then she added, rather pointedly, "But we welcome that same kind from other places, as long as they live up to that mold." She couldn't stop herself from giving him a wry smile. "Even if some of us are slower on the uptake."

He shrugged. "You had your reasons, and they were . . . understandable assumptions."

"Just wrong ones."

A slight smile curved his mouth. That darned mouth. "Thank you. I appreciate that. But . . . could we maybe put that behind us?"

A bigger smile spread over her face. "Consider it in the rearview mirror."

He chuckled, and she felt as if she'd accomplished something . . . nice. For a long moment their gazes locked, and it was as if the entire atmosphere had shifted. As if the air itself had suddenly come alive, crackling with energy. As if whatever had triggered that flash of sudden heat had struck once more, only magnified tenfold. Perhaps because this time it was going both ways. She had this sudden vision of two bolts of lightning colliding and energizing all the air around them.

And she belatedly considered the words she'd spoken. If her misjudgment of him was in the rearview mirror, then where were they headed now?

She pushed the thoughts aside, which, even as she did it,

she admitted was unlike her. She was more a "confront the issue now" kind of person, and this wasn't like her. But here she was burying deep the very thing she should be addressing.

She felt the need to run, to escape, and was mortified by the urge. She wasn't someone who ran away from her problems. She just wasn't quite ready for the insanity of wanting to kiss Jackson Thorpe.

She scrambled for another subject, any other subject, and they chatted amiably enough to slow her racing pulse. She kept on until that moment, that electrifying instant, had faded before saying something about having an early lesson in the morning and getting to her feet.

"Say good night to Jeremy for me?"

"Of course."

She started to take her mug to the kitchen, but he politely told her to leave it, he'd get it. He walked her to the door, as any good host would. Opened it for her. She stepped out onto the porch, noticing with some surprise it was already nearly sunset.

She turned to thank him for the coffee and say good night. In the same instant, he stepped out onto the porch himself, and they collided. He was as solid as she would have expected, if such close contact had ever been allowed into her mind. Okay, other than in the dreams she couldn't seem to fight off.

His lips parted as if he were about to speak, but no words

came. But those lips were suddenly all she could see.

She kissed him.

She kissed him and he tasted so warm, the hint of coffee lingering, his lips firm yet giving, and even though she had to stretch upward to reach, she couldn't make herself pull away. And for a long, sweet, intense moment, neither did he. In fact, for that moment he kissed her back, as if . . . as if he'd wanted this too. Or at least had wondered what it would be like.

Had he expected this . . . deluge of sensation? Or was it just her responding so fiercely? Had it just been too long for her, or had her body been aware of something her mind had shoved aside? Had some part of her known it would be like this?

It was Jackson who finally broke the kiss, who pulled back. She was almost afraid to look at him, afraid she'd see distaste in those famous eyes. But she saw nothing but surprise—that she'd dared?—and . . . heat. That same heat that had crackled between them before, in that brief, intense moment when their gazes had locked.

The sound of Jeremy's voice did what her own will had not been able to—jolted her back to reality.

"You leavin'?" the boy asked. And only then did she realize that this was why Jackson had broken the kiss. He must have heard the boy coming down the ladder. If he hadn't, would he have kept on, made it deeper, sweeter?

She had to swallow before she could speak. "Yes. I would

have come up to say good night, but I didn't want to interrupt your homework. Or"—she glanced at his father— "your book selection."

"That's okay. I'm almost done." He, too, glanced at his father, and added almost shyly, "And I already picked out the book."

"Good night, then," she said.

"Go finish," Jackson told the boy. "Then I'll be up. Maybe with some hot chocolate, huh?"

"Cool," Jeremy said, throwing a "'Night," at her over his shoulder.

"Good night to you too," she said when the boy had gone.

"Very good," he said, his voice a little rough, sending a little shiver through her. "Much better than I expected."

This time he kissed her, leaning in and practically blanking out every rational thought she'd recovered in the last minute. And when she was back home, in front of her wing of the main house, she sat in her car, her forehead resting on the steering wheel, eyes closed, as she relived those moments on his porch.

When she opened her eyes again, it was nearly dark. And she went inside with the certain knowledge that she'd be having one of those dreams tonight.

Chapter Twenty-Five

G OBSMACKED.

Jackson didn't know where the word originated, but it was the only one that fit how he felt.

He shifted restlessly on the bed he had, up until now, been sleeping well on. He'd thought he would tonight, as well, after the fun of reading from Jeremy's favorite book to him again. But here he was, stuck in a morass of tangled thoughts.

For two years he'd never even thought about getting close to another woman. Even though he'd had his instructions from Leah.

If anything happens to one of us, the other needs to move on.

She'd said it after finishing a book that had obviously gotten to her. He'd been scrambling, trying to think of something to reply to the unexpectedly intense comment when the Leah he so loved had emerged, with that impish smile that made him smile back no matter what was going on.

But if you ever do it while I'm still alive, I'll kill you.

They'd ended up making long, sweet love right there on the sofa she'd been curled up on. He'd thought often of that night and was still convinced that was the night Jeremy had been conceived. Just the memory of her words always caused that pain somewhere down deep, as if it had been physically able to deliver a blow. He waited for the punch.

It didn't come.

Instead, all he felt was a wistful sadness, not even about how much he missed her, but how much she was missing. She wasn't seeing Jeremy grow, seeing how much and how fast he was learning.

She couldn't see the change in him since they'd come here.

But somehow he knew she'd approve. She'd approve of anything that helped their son.

Even Nic?

Because he couldn't deny she was helping Jeremy. The boy was never more excited than when he was aboard Pie, and more than once he'd paused in his day to watch, and had seen both of them laughing with delight over some leap of progress in his riding.

Nic told me it was okay to be mad about Mom being gone. That she was mad her mom got hurt, 'n' if she'd died, like my mom did, it'd be a bazillion times worse.

He remembered that evening, when that had come out over a bowl of ice cream before bed. He hadn't really thought about what else Jeremy and Nic might be talking about in their time together, but he should have. When the boy was actually riding, that was the focus, but there was all that time when he was grooming Pie or cleaning the tack or the pony's stall, all part of the privilege of riding, according to the Nicole Baylor method. All that time to talk about . . . anything. Which they apparently did.

She said when she got really sad about her mom never being able to walk again, she'd ride out to one of her favorite places. An' just stay there, looking, until she felt better.

He understood that. Leah would have understood that.

Would she have understood that kiss?

If anything happens to one of us, the other needs to move on.

Maybe. Maybe she would have understood. Even approve. Because anyone who could make Jeremy happy the way Nic did, especially now, would be okay in Leah's book.

"I'll never stop loving you, Leah," he murmured into the darkness, as if he felt like he had to reassure her. Why? Because of that kiss?

Or because that kiss was just the first step? The first step on a path he'd never thought he'd walk again . . .

He rolled over, giving the pillow beneath his head a solid punch. The constant ache of losing Leah had become part of him, and he wasn't sure how he felt about it easing. Guilty, perhaps. Did it belittle what they'd had if he did what she'd said and moved on? Or was he a beaten, helpless washout who couldn't function at all without the woman who had been his support, who had kept him sane in a crazy world?

When he finally fell asleep, it was to dream of Leah as he often did, yet this dream was different. It began, as usual, with something entirely unrelated, something about being in Last Stand in the old days, just after the battle. But then, dressed for the period, Leah appeared. She was farther away than usual, and the image of her was a bit fuzzy around the edges. He felt Jeremy's hand in his, but couldn't tear his gaze away to look at him.

The dream image said something, faintly, and Jeremy pulled on his hand as he asked, "What did she say?"

"She said . . . let me go."

He woke up abruptly, jerking half upright before he even realized he'd been asleep. His heart was racing, and he felt a bit clammy.

Let me go.

He didn't believe in supernatural stuff like messages from beyond, or the afterlife, or whatever they called it.

But he had no other explanation for this.

THERE HAD BEEN an underlying hum of tension between them ever since that evening. Nic didn't know if it was coincidence or intent—on his part or even hers—but they weren't alone together for more than a moment or two for the next couple of days. And when they were, it was always in the middle of a job or some work that required all hands.

And work was something the man couldn't seem to get enough of. He seemed to be taking on more and more, and when she'd told him he didn't have to work quite that hard, he simply said he wanted to learn. She'd believed it . . . until Maggie Rafferty had mentioned she'd told him about Dad's heart attack. The timing lined up too perfectly to deny. He was taking on more work to help her father.

Which only makes you like him even more.

She'd just reached the point of accepting that fact when her mother dropped a figurative bomb on them. But, being Mom, she disguised it cleverly.

"If it's all right with you, Jackson," she'd said when he'd come down to watch the end of Jeremy's riding lesson for the day and she was there, "Jeremy's going to spend the evening with us. One of my favorite riding-related movies is on, and he wants to see it."

"I . . . sure."

It was unlike Mom to not invite him to stay as well, and that was Nic's tip-off that something else was up. So, when it hit, she wasn't surprised. Not that that stopped her pulse from kicking into overdrive.

"Jeremy can stay overnight. We've already discussed it, and he's fine with it. So why don't you two go out on the town? Jackson, you haven't been to the saloon on a Friday night yet, have you? You can't be an official Last Stander until you do that."

And that simply, they'd both been maneuvered. They either had to do it, or one of them had to come up with a decent excuse to get out of it. Except . . . she didn't want to get out of it. But maybe he did. Maybe he regretted those moments on the porch, regretted that kiss that had so blown her away. If he did, she wanted to know now, before she did anything stupid.

Well, more stupid than kissing him.

But then he kissed you . . .

He had. And it had lit her up from head to toe. And so she simply looked at him, clearly handing the decision over to him.

It was a moment before he switched his gaze from her mother to her. Just long enough, she guessed, to let Mom know he saw through her ploy. But when he did look at her, she couldn't read his expression at all.

He's an actor. He can probably turn that utterly neutral expression on and off at will.

But that would mean he'd meant her to see his response to her kiss. Or the flash of heat that had inspired her to take the reckless step. Or had he been so far away from his work in that moment that the actor part of him hadn't even been present? She'd like to believe that.

When he finally spoke, it wasn't what she'd expected at all.

"Do I have to dress up for this?"

Chapter Twenty-Six

"H E'S NOTHING LIKE I expected."
    "He's really nice."
"He seems genuine, not fake."

The pronouncements kept coming at her, usually delivered in whispers even though the subject of them was on the far side of the saloon. Was, in fact, engaged in a game of pool with Last Stand's unexpected pool shark, Joey Highwater. As usual when Joey played, a crowd had gathered to watch, but this time Nic was sure who she was playing was the main reason the crowd was so big. And she couldn't help noticing the locals had come together in sort of a human wall, keeping the strangers a bit at bay, able to look and gawk, but not bother.

Last Stand was protecting him.

As for all the people making those comments to her—she had to keep telling herself it was because he was living on the Baylor ranch, not because they suspected anything was going on between them, or because she had atypically dressed up, in her favorite, rather slinky blue dress—she only nodded and confirmed, "I know the feeling. I was as surprised as you are. But yes, he's for real."

And when she'd had to admit it to Jessica, who was gawking as much as anyone at the pool match going on, her friend had the grace to say, "I knew you'd get over it."

It was the one who asked, "Do you think he'll stay?" that stirred up the unease in her stomach now. Not only because of the question, but because of who asked it. Kane Highwater, who had unexpectedly shown up. She knew he'd just gotten back from a southwest tour, which, by all accounts, had been a rousing success, spreading the incredible music of the young artist beyond Texas. His story was so exceptional, it only added to the mystique. And she'd often wondered if, after his years of wandering, tortured by an undeserved guilt, he would be able to stay in any one place for long.

And over there was Jackson Thorpe, tortured by an undeserved death, and she was wondering the same thing about him.

"Maybe I should ask you that," she suggested quietly. "You know what it's like to have your life forever changed by the death of someone you loved. Although he"—she nodded toward the pool table—"isn't carrying around a load of undeserved guilt over it."

"Behind me now," the youngest Highwater son said with a shrug. "Thanks to Lark," he added. "She's sorry she couldn't make it tonight. She had an appointment with some adopting parents." He said it with such emotion in his resonant voice it made her ache inside. Not in the way it once had, wondering what it must feel like to be so in love, but in the way of someone who suddenly thinks it just might be possible.

The very thought made her edgy. This was Jackson Thorpe she was thinking about, the guy so famous that, now that word had gotten out he was here, had the saloon filled wall to wall, with most of the crowd straining for just a glimpse of him.

In an effort to get her recalcitrant mind off this track, she joked, "My money's on Joey."

"Mine too," Kane said with a grin that put her in mind of his stage presence, when that wiry, lightning-quick way of moving he had seemed to spark an energy in his audience that was unlike anything she'd seen live before. And then he opened up and that voice poured out—"And on him staying," Kane added, derailing her thoughts.

She turned her head to stare at him. He shrugged again. "One of the things I learned in my years on the move was to recognize the people who weren't, the ones who were home. He's got that look, Nic."

As he walked away, headed on a beeline to Lark, his words echoed in her mind as so often his songs did, capturing the essence of something so completely, it filled the heart. She watched Jackson as the game progressed, saw the way he laughed, how the others around him joined in, some even good-naturedly teasing him, and he taking it in the same vein. He looked like nothing different than a guy out with friends. Friends he trusted.

"That is a lot happier man than the Jackson Thorpe I first met."

She turned to see Slater Highwater, who had walked up to where she was leaning against the bar.

"Yes," she said, allowing herself to believe it. "Yes, I think he is."

"He's a good fit. He should stay."

Okay, that was two Highwaters vouching for him staying. She had the feeling Keller and Maggie Rafferty would also agree. With votes from two of the founding families of Last Stand, it was practically a done deal.

If he wanted it.

WITH A SHOCK Jackson realized that the small ache in his ribs wasn't from working, although he'd been doing a lot he wasn't used to, it was from . . . laughing. It had been a very long time since he'd laughed this much. Or enjoyed an evening this much. Not just since Leah had been killed, but even before, when the sudden burst of fame that had enveloped him had made it nearly impossible to have a night like this back in L.A.

Yet here he was, deep into a game of pool with, of all people, the helpful librarian. And if he was honest, she was going to beat his ass. He glanced around at the grinning people closest to the table, the ones who had egged him into this contest. Keller Rafferty, and the artist brother he'd just met tonight, Rylan, who had made the belt Jeremy so loved. He'd been a little nervous when Rylan had introduced his wife, Kaitlyn, mentioning she was a photographer. But the woman had picked up on it immediately and whispered quietly to him, "You're safe, don't even have a phone camera on me."

He'd blinked, but smiled despite himself. "Thanks."

"I wouldn't, anyway. You're off duty here, as it were."

He was diverted by the amazing idea that maybe, just maybe, this was a place where he could be the guy he'd once been, and not the superstar Hollywood had made him—whether he liked it or not—simply for doing the one thing he was best at.

Sometimes he thought this place was too good to be true.

Then he caught a glimpse of Nic in that almost shiny blue dress she'd worn tonight, that little number that flowed down over her curves and flipped sassily up at the bottom, a couple of inches above her knees on those long, long legs. And that totally distracted him from what he was doing. So much so that he missed his shot, and essentially handed the game to Joey. And judging by the whoops from the encircling group, they all knew it.

The sexy librarian—and saloonkeeper's wife—cleared the felt of stripes with one last shot. As the gathering cheered, Jackson put on his most humble expression and bowed to her, his cue held out crossways on his palms as if he were a knight offering his sword in surrender.

It went over well, the crowd cheered, and Joey said in regal tones, "You may rise." Then she grinned at him and said, "Nice game."

Slater came up and slipped his arm around his wife. "Indeed," he agreed, looking at Jackson. "Now you should get back to your lady." He nodded back toward the bar.

His lady?

He turned, and Nic was right there on the edge of the crowd, in that damn dress. She smiled, not the quick surface smile of a casual connecting of glances, but a warm, slow smile that made his pulse kick up with an almost audible thump.

He turned back to excuse himself and saw Joey watching him while her husband was talking to someone he hadn't met yet.

"She's the real deal," Joey said quietly enough that only he would hear amid the steady hum of the crowd. "Honest, loyal, generous, and as dedicated to the work she loves as you are. And it's that you work so hard that matters, not what that work is."

"That was . . . quite an assessment."

She grinned. "I judge people by how they behave in the library."

"Good a way as any." His own returning grin faded when he asked, deadly serious, "But what made you think I needed to know that?"

Just as seriously as his own words had been, she said, "Because in all the years I've known her, I've never seen her look at a man the way she looks at you."

He drew back slightly, tried to swallow past the sudden tightness of his throat.

"And," Joey added, that impish grin returning, "at least you know it's not some surface fan infatuation, not after the way she treated you when you first got here."

He hadn't thought about it quite like that, but she had a point. There had been no denying Nic's opinion of him when he'd arrived. Or that it had changed over the course of the month—had it really only been a month?—he'd been here in Last Stand.

"Shoo," Joey said, then went to join her husband.

And Jackson headed for Nic.

Chapter Twenty-Seven

S HE WATCHED HIM stride across the room toward her, and people cleared his way as if he had some magical power. A ridiculous thought, but the first one that came to her. And in that moment, she could see him as any fictional hero she could think of, and making it work. Maybe that was why it worked, because at the core, he was who he was, and that didn't change, just as it didn't in the character he played. It was only the trappings that changed. The heart was pure hero.

She remembered what he'd said about never having played—or wanting to—a bad guy, and she could see now why. Because no one would ever believe this man was evil at heart. She'd been misled by her own assumptions, and it had kept her from seeing the man behind the role, the real man.

But she saw him now.

And when he suggested they get out of the crowd, she never hesitated.

They'd come in his rental SUV. He'd said he'd gotten to where he could find his way around in daylight, mostly, but nighttime was another experience altogether and he needed to learn.

"You actually have nighttime here," he'd said. "I've for-gotten how dark it is without a gazillion city lights to wipe it out."

"Do you miss it?" she'd asked.

That was when, his hand on the gearshift, he'd turned to meet her gaze head-on. "Not. One. Bit."

Whether it was the way he said it, each one-syllable word with such emphasis, or the way he'd looked at her when he did, she didn't know, but she felt a flood of such warmth she quickly turned away, afraid of what might be showing in her face.

And now, as they drove through that darkness, she pon-dered. It was strange for her to feel so uncertain. She never had before. She tried to write it off to how she'd felt about him in the beginning, how she'd disliked him on principle. But now that she knew better . . . she didn't know what to chalk the emotions he stirred in her up to.

Well, except for the obvious, of course. That she'd fallen in with a few million women across the country who were infatuated with actor Jackson Thorpe.

She gave him a quick sideways glance and shook off that thought easily now. Because when she looked at him, she didn't see the actor who'd stolen hearts across the country. She saw the guy who had walked away from the kind of stardom others would kill for, for the sake of his son. The guy who had moved halfway across the country in the hopes it would help his son. The guy who, even though he could well afford to do nothing, hated the idea and essentially worked as a ranch hand, because he wanted to. And because it helped her father.

That was the man she'd fallen for.

Her breath caught as the words formed in her mind. Had she? Really?

She tried to put out of her mind who he was—or had been, before he'd come to Last Stand—and picture what it might have been like if she'd met him someplace like the feedstore. Or the bookstore, knowing him now. She was honest enough to admit that just his looks would have caught her eye. The voice would still have hit that spot deep down that set up an echoing vibration in her. And the eyes . . . well, she could admit those deep-blue eyes would have had her wondering what it would be like if they heated up looking at her.

And she could admit that, if he'd been a local, or a Hill Country guy, or even just a Texan, she would have been immediately interested. Very interested.

So what was she now?

When they arrived at the ranch, seeing that all the lights in the house were out, she gave a startled glance at the clock in the dash of the vehicle. She couldn't quite believe it was after midnight.

He pulled up in front of her wing of the house. When he shut the engine off, it seemed almost unnaturally quiet, especially after the constant buzz of a Friday night at the Last Stand Saloon. He unfastened his seat belt, then turned in the driver's seat to look at her. And waited.

And suddenly, that quiet was alive, humming between them as if he'd said something startling. Shocking. Suggestive? Was he waiting to be invited in? If he was, would she invite him?

Nicole Baylor was not an indecisive person. She'd always known what she wanted in life and went after it. But now she couldn't seem to speak or move. And Jackson was just . . . looking at her. Waiting.

She groaned inwardly. She had to get away from him. She couldn't think straight when he was *right there*. Almost on her thought, he turned away and opened his door. She was a little stunned at how empty the vehicle suddenly felt, and it took her a moment to realize he'd walked around to open the passenger door for her. She ordered herself to snap out of it. She belatedly undid her own seat belt and turned to get out. She was not used to such uncertainty and, somewhat embarrassedly had to admit she didn't know what to do.

There was another frozen moment, with her staring up into those eyes, trying to read him. And for that moment, he was looking at her the same way, assessingly, as if he were trying to gauge if she—

He stepped back, and the cold night air rushed in between them. She'd waited too long. And as if the chill had numbed her, she silently walked to her front door, regret already bubbling beneath the surface.

Why couldn't she find the words? True, she hadn't been in this situation for a very long time, alone with a man she was attracted to—okay, beyond attracted, a man she flat-out wanted—with nothing to keep them from pursuing this heat that seemed to spark between them. She had kissed him once, and he had kissed her back, after all. But now he politely followed and waited, like the gentleman he obviously was at heart, until she had it open.

So here she stood, Nicole Baylor, well-known trainer who'd dealt with some contrary horses in her time, including one pretty ornery stud, and she had no idea what to do. And thinking of Jackson in conjunction with that fiery stallion, who knew exactly what his purpose in life was, completely derailed any logical thought process.

He leaned in and whispered something she was too befuddled at the moment to process. And it wasn't until he was back in the SUV and headed up the hill that the words—and the meaning—registered.

If you change your mind, you know where I am.

She watched the taillights recede, then vanish at the turn toward the hill house.

If you change your mind, you know where I am.

That had to mean he felt the same, didn't it?

For a moment she almost wished he was one of those guys who'd try to convince her with a swarm of kisses and touches until she was too hot to say no. But for all that he came out of Hollywood, he obviously was not one of those. He'd been a perfect gentleman, a Texas gentleman, as her mother would have said.

Her mother. Who had orchestrated this whole night. Who had sent them out together, hoping for . . . what? What had Mom hoped to accomplish?

The answer should have hit her back when Mom had first said it, which was a measure of how disconcerted she was. Because it was crystal clear, now.

Jeremy can stay overnight . . .

Also belatedly, it hit her that Jackson could have gone in and gotten Jeremy to take him home. But he hadn't. He'd left him here, with her folks, and headed home. Alone. The only night alone he'd had since he'd arrived.

And who knew when there'd ever be another one? There might never be another chance like this one.

Chapter Twenty-Eight

JACKSON REGRETTED WHAT he'd said the moment the words came out, not because he hadn't meant them—because he certainly, breathlessly had—but because he was sure what he thought he'd seen in her had been wishful thinking. She hadn't really looked at him like she'd wanted him to kiss her again.

She probably regretted the first time. She probably wished he'd just back off. Probably thought he expected her to crumple at his feet just because of who he was. He knew she'd thought that of him in the beginning. But now?

Could we maybe put that behind us?

Consider it in the rearview mirror.

Didn't that sort of imply they were moving . . . ahead?

He gave a sharp shake of his head as he parked the car and went inside. The spacious, vaulted great room which had seemed welcoming before echoed a bit hollowly now. Amazing how much space one little boy could fill, both inside this building and inside his heart.

They needed that dog. Keller had promised to call as soon as his brother got home. Chance Rafferty and his wife were off to rescue yet another military K9 deemed unsalvageable. He'd looked up the website for *They Also Serve* and been impressed with both Chance and the mission.

Another Texas man stepping up.

He hung up his jacket, walked over to the kitchen, and tossed his keys on the counter. That put him standing in front of the upper cabinet, where, when they'd moved in and he'd been checking to see if the necessary utensils for what home cooking he did—he'd learned a bit since Leah had died and he'd had to—were there, and he'd found an unopened bottle of tequila.

He pulled it out now, contemplating. Wondered, as he did now and then, if those weeks of losing himself in booze meant he could never have a drink again. He studied the label. *Outlaw Tequila*, read the label. And he remembered driving by a location with a sign saying just that on their way to the saloon. Directly behind the saloon, in fact. Convenient, considering the amount he'd seen Slater Highwater pouring tonight.

At least it's not mescal.

Then again, that might be better, because he wouldn't be thinking about drinking it, not with the worm. Which was really the larva of some bug or other. Which, in turn, did not make it any more appealing.

He grimaced, remembering again that video Tris had shot of him, drunk on his ass with his then barely five-year-old son trying to take care of him. He put the bottle back in the cupboard. Maybe when Jeremy turned eighteen . . .

He was trying to picture that when the quiet tap came on the door, and so his first thought was the boy had awakened in a strange room and had wanted to come home. Funny how he'd never had any problem here, in the loft. He'd loved this place since he'd first set foot through the door, and Jackson had to admit he had the same feeling.

He pulled open the door, expecting his son. Instead, he saw Nic, looking up at him with those gray-blue eyes, which seemed bright even in the faint glow of the light from inside flowing out onto the porch. The jacket she wore hung off one shoulder, as if she'd yanked it on in a hurry. She was breathing rather quickly, and he told himself it was because she'd just hiked that half mile here. The logical part of his brain that knew what kind of shape she was in laughed at that.

He felt as if he'd taken a step into a minefield where anything he said could blow this up, so he said nothing. He just stared down at her, the air around them suddenly so charged, his skin started to tingle.

"I'd already made up my mind," she said, her voice low and husky, and the tingle became a shiver of anticipation. "I just had to give my heart a pep talk. It wasn't sure it was ready."

"Neither was mine, but it got outvoted."

He heard her short little intake of breath before she said, "Then we have a decision?"

"And all night to enact it," he said gruffly. Then, with a

grimace, he said, "I'm not exactly . . . prepared for this. Protection wise, I mean."

"I am," she said, and he hoped the look she gave him meant it counted as a point in his favor that he'd been the one to bring it up. She reached into her jacket pocket and pulled out a box of condoms. At his look she grimaced slightly. "Mom. Her subtle way of suggesting I need to get out more."

"And here you are," he said softly.

"Here I am." She reached up and laid her palm flat on his chest, over his heart. "You're . . . sure?"

He put his hand over hers. "I'm sure. For the first time in two years, I'm sure."

She stared at him. "You can't mean you haven't . . . since she died . . ."

"Tried once. Disaster. Because it was for all the wrong reasons." He took a steadying breath. He wasn't quite sure why he was driven to go on, but he was. "I didn't really . . . care. About her. I didn't admire her. Respect her. Believe in her. Trust her."

He saw her eyes start to glisten, even in the shadows. And knew she hadn't missed the implication of what he'd said. That he did feel all those things about her. The question was, was that enough for her? Because he didn't love her. That capacity still lay buried beneath a headstone back in L.A.

But want her?

Oh, yeah. For the first time since Leah's death, he could answer that with a fervent yes and mean it. Already his body had awakened at the idea.

A different sort of awareness flickered through him, that sense of guilt he'd always felt at even thinking about being with another woman. But it was followed immediately by the memory of that dream. Or whatever it had been.

Let me go.

Then Tris's advice, born out of awful, painful experience, rang in his head. *You'll always love her, bro. But you can't be in love* with *her, because that takes two.*

And he realized he had one more thing to do, before he took a step toward accepting what she was apparently offering. He owed her that much. He tried to think of some tactful way to say it, but in the end, it came out bluntly.

"I can't love you. I don't think I'll ever really love again."

Something flared for a split second in her eyes, but it vanished, replaced by that impish Nic smile he actually did love. "Revoking the invitation?"

"No," he said hastily. "God, no. I just . . . wanted to be honest."

"And that," she said, moving her hand up to cup his cheek, "is all I ask."

The rush of relief he felt, that she didn't turn and walk away after what he'd said, surprised him. But from the moment she stepped inside, there was no room for anything except the fire she lit in him. She stretched up to kiss him, and it quickly blossomed into the hottest kiss he could ever have imagined. He wanted more, he wanted her closer, and he backed up to lean against the wall so he could slide down a little, to be level with that mouth of hers that was driving him utterly mad. She went with him eagerly, straddling him, and he had a sudden vision of her riding him, naked and hot, and he nearly lost it right then.

And after that kiss, he finally believed this was really going to happen, and he went a little mad. He wasn't sure whose clothes he was tearing at half the time, and Nic met his every move with one of her own to accomplish the same. And he finally got his wish, to see that long, thick fall of silken hair loosed and free, flowing halfway down her back and brushing over his own skin in a way that made him shiver.

They went to the floor, still half-dressed, and after an awkward fumble with the condom box he didn't even care about, he let loose the fierce attraction he'd apparently been bottling since he'd first laid eyes on her. She shifted to make it easier for him to slide into her, without ever stopping that string of long, deep kisses that had his heart ready to burst out of his chest, it was hammering so hard.

Her hot, slick flesh welcomed him, and he slid deep. He heard a gasp, a groan of pleasure, and he wasn't even sure who it came from. And then she was moving, taking him deeper, and he barely managed to hang on until he heard her moan and her body clenched around him. He ground out an oath that was as much tribute to her as to the overpowering wave of sensation that swamped him as he poured himself into her.

And as they lay there, entangled, he had the strangest feeling more than just pent-up desire had been released between them.

Chapter Twenty-Nine

N IC EYED THE approaching clouds warily. They were big enough and dark enough for her to believe they were going to get their average of two inches of rain for February all in one go. It was unusual for a storm of the predicted magnitude to hit them this early in the year, but not unheard of, so they weren't taking any chances.

She again ran through her mental list of things that needed to be done, to make sure she'd hit them all. She'd been running full tilt since the warning had come in from Cody Rafferty's uncannily accurate weather drones that the storm had changed course and was headed their way. The youngest Rafferty brother was a tech whiz, and he had made ranch life in the Hill Country easier with this system and his fence monitoring system that not only warned you if you had a breach, but told you exactly where it was, which saved at least two or three days of work on the bigger ranches, where there were miles of fence line to ride.

Bigger, like we used to be.

She smothered a sigh. They were doing fine, better than they had for a while, since they'd sold that chunk off. She had reached the realization that, in the end, it had been a wise decision. And at least it had been sold to someone they trusted not to turn it into some overpopulated neighborhood of condos and expensive coffee vendors. Riley Garrett was a rancher to the soles of her worn boots, and ever would be, and had promised they could buy it back if they ever wanted to.

It was just that she dreaded ever facing that kind of decision again, when they might have to give up more, just to stay afloat. Or a time when the skills they had to offer were no longer valued. But for now, they were fine, even doing well, and she would just have to focus on that.

And the simple fact that she was head over heels for the guy who was helping make that possible by insisting on paying rent, even with all the work he did. Her cheeks heated a little as she remembered yesterday, when Dad had nearly caught them stealing a kiss in the tack room. It wasn't that she was hiding this from them—in fact, she suspected Mom at least knew perfectly well what was going on, given that she had facilitated it—but she wasn't quite ready to share it. Yet. After a week it still felt new, and somehow clandestine, because they had only the hours when Jeremy was with Mom to steal any time together. Which took today out of the mix, since it was Saturday.

Besides, they hadn't told Jeremy yet, and it seemed to her he should be the first one to know, officially. Assuming, of course, it lasted long enough he needed to be told. After all, Jackson had already told her he couldn't love her. She knew why, she even understood. But she couldn't help wondering how she'd ended up feeling envious of a dead woman.

He couldn't love her, and she didn't want to love him. No, she needed some steady, ranch-loving Texas man who wasn't above dedicating himself to what it took to keep a ranch going.

But isn't Jackson doing just that?

She grimaced inwardly. Because he was doing that, she just wasn't sure how long he'd be happy about it. And that thought conflicted with her insistence that she didn't want to love him, which collided with the fact that he couldn't love her. It was such a tangle, she didn't know how to begin to sort it out.

But she did care, about both him and Jeremy. A lot. More than she could remember caring about any other man before. But it wasn't love. It just wasn't. It couldn't be. Infatuation, maybe. That she could accept, but she couldn't afford to give her heart away to a guy who might get bored with the life she loved at any moment.

She didn't usually look for trouble, not when so much arrived on its own without her help, but as with so many things with him, this was different. She was different with him, and it rattled her.

Then the sound of distant thunder snapped her out of her useless meanderings.

Focus, Baylor. That thunderstorm's almost here.

Once she was through her mental checklist and certain

she'd done everything, that the livestock were in the more protected pastures, the horses secure in the barn—including Jeremy's precious Pie—and everything battened down as best it could be, she headed in. And arrived just in time to see an expensive European sedan pulling away from the house.

"Who was that?" Nic asked as she watched the car head up the hill. Toward Jackson. She looked back at her parents, who were on the porch, also watching it go, and neither of them looked happy.

"That," her father said flatly, "was some Hollywood bigwig who came to see Jackson."

"To talk him into going back, you mean," her mother said, her tone beyond sour.

Nic felt her stomach give a sudden churn. "Going back?"

"Yes," Mom said. "He as much as said they'd given him more than a month to get his head right, and it was time for him to get back to work."

And Nic had the sinking feeling that there was more than one kind of storm on the immediate horizon. What would he do? Had he found enough here to hold him? How could anybody in his position refuse such a demand?

Was she about to lose him, when she'd barely begun to learn all the facets of him?

The doubts she'd thought vanquished rose yet again; how could she, a simple ranch girl from small-town Texas, hold a man like Jackson Thorpe?

She was very afraid she knew the answer to that.

She couldn't.

JACKSON TOED OFF his boots—which had become more battered in a month of real ranch life than they had in five years of portraying it, which he supposed told him something—and hung up his jacket. Nic's dad had been anxious to get everything prepared for this massive storm rolling in to remind them, Richard had said, that winter wasn't quite over yet. Between them they'd gotten everything loose at the barn under cover, the hay secured, all doors secured, and the generator checked, fueled, and tested. Nic had been out moving the last group of the Angus into the smaller, higher pasture, away from the creek that could flood if the rain stayed as intense as forecast, but she should be done by now.

For a moment he just stood there, staring at that spot just inside the door. He was still surprised at himself. It hit him every time he thought back over the week that had begun that first night with Nic. He'd never expected it to be so . . . much. So overpowering, so incredible.

He'd thought he'd feel guilty if he ever had sex again, with someone else, after Leah. Especially if he enjoyed it.

Enjoyed it? Hell, he'd about gone through the roof. Again, and again, as if he'd stored up all the longing and need of those years and let it loose all at once.

Or Nic battered down the walls and freed it.

That was closer to the truth. From the moment she'd stepped inside that first night and kissed him, it had been full speed ahead. It was clear once Nicole Baylor made up her mind, she didn't second-guess. They hadn't even made it to the bed until the third time. If she hadn't had a training session and he hadn't needed to check on Jeremy, he could have easily and happily spent the entire day in bed with her. Now, after a week of stolen hours together, it was just as hot, just as amazing. More, actually, as they learned each other.

And he still got that tightness in his throat and chest when he watched her with Jeremy. This, at least, he knew Leah would approve of. She would be for anything that was good for their precious little boy. And Nic was very, very good for Jeremy. Even now, when he was used to it, watching his son laugh when Nic got him going, watching his pride in his riding skills as she nurtured them, never failed to reach him, deeply.

So now the boy was no doubt still down in the barn where he'd left him to finish up on his brushing Pie yet one more time, even though the little pinto pony was already gleaming. The last time he'd walked by the stall, Jeremy was talking to the animal about next week's riding lessons, which Nic had promised him would be outside the corral, learning how to adjust for going up and down steeper hillsides, and fording the creek.

He'd told Jeremy to head up here as soon as he was done, but now realized he should have been more time-specific, because if the kid had his way, he'd never be done with that pony, who seemed to have decided the adoration was mutual. Jackson was pondering going down to get the boy into the house before the storm hit when he heard the sound of a car pulling up outside. His first thought was Nic, but then it usually was. But it wasn't her truck. No, this had a quieter, more civilized sound to it, and when he looked out the window, he saw why; he hadn't seen one of those since he'd left L.A. The sleek European sedan looked out of place, but he didn't have time to dwell on that when he saw who was driving it.

Felix Swiff. Head executive producer and backer of *Stonewall*. The big guy. The money and power guy. A guy who didn't make casual trips just to visit. If he was here, it was only for one reason. He was going to put the pressure on.

Damn.

For a moment he actually considered not opening the door. Pretending he wasn't here. Maybe the big storm heading in would drive the man back to L.A.

Now that'd be a great example for Jeremy, wouldn't it?

He headed for the door.

"Quaint place you've got here," Swiff said the moment he opened it.

He was sure Swiff thought so, given the sharp-edged, uber-modern mansion in the Hollywood Hills the man lived in. He had nothing really against Swiff, only that he represented the money side of the business that Jackson, perhaps foolishly, didn't want to get into any more deeply than he had to. Well, that, and his fairly autocratic ways.

Jackson lifted a brow at him. And didn't move aside for him to come in. "Shouldn't you be out playing golf or something?"

"I'm not here to talk about where I should be, but where you should be. We've stalled and tap-danced around it for as long as we can, Jackson. You need to come home."

The moment Swiff said it, Jackson felt a jab as if the man had tried to punch him. And the only words that fit the feeling were, *I am home.*

Somehow that gave him the strength to step aside and—intentionally, rather grandly—wave Swiff inside. "Come on in and say your piece, Felix." *Even though it won't do you any good.*

Swiff started with flattery. "Look, I'll admit it. The show isn't doing well without you. The ratings have, frankly, tanked since we had to send Austin Holt away on some fictional mission. Especially when viewers know at least some version of the truth, that you walked away."

Jackson knew this from Tucker, but Jeremy was his priority, and the change that he'd seen in his son since they'd come here outweighed anything Swiff could possibly say. "I understand and I'm sorry, Felix. But I was losing my son. I had to get him out of there. And this was the only place he wanted to be."

"And I understand that," Swiff said, although his total lack of a relationship with his own now-adult children made Jackson doubt if he really did. "But think about all the other people, and their kids, that you're hurting, Jackson. There are people depending on you, not just the other actors, but the crew, the wranglers, the stunt team, including your friend, Tucker."

And that was Jackson's weak point, because those were the people he most didn't want to hurt. But he had to put Jeremy's welfare above all else. Right now, painful though the thought of other damage he was doing might be, nothing mattered more than his little boy.

Finally, Swiff went to the big gun, the thing Jackson had been expecting. He suspected it was coming when Swiff started pacing the floor. When he finally stopped—although oddly, Jackson thought he heard another couple of steps even after Swiff had stopped moving—it came out in grim, flat tones. "You're under contract, Jackson."

"I know that."

"That means legal ramifications if you insist on this."

"You do what you have to do."

"I don't want to have to force you. This could cost you a great deal, including your entire future in this business. You have no choice. You have to come back."

Jackson heard that sound from the porch again, the wind no doubt, as the storm got close. But he ignored it as Swiff delivered the ultimatum in a flat, brook-no-denial kind of tone. And in that moment, Jackson considered yet again what he was giving up. Weighed it against the change in his son, from the child who never even smiled to the joyous boy who grinned widely as he rode that pony. Who even came home from his lessons excited and eager to talk about all he was learning.

The scales leaned so far to one side, there wasn't really any decision to make.

But Swiff took his silence in a different way, saying briskly, "Good. I'll make the arrangements for your return and tell the writers they can bring Austin back. And I'd better call the publicists, they'll need to get started. Welcome back, Jackson."

Jackson opened his mouth to correct Swiff's misapprehension; he wasn't going anywhere. He knew what he'd be bringing on. There was no way the businessman could understand walking away from a gold mine like *Stonewall*. He'd erupt. And it just might cost Jackson everything. Lawyers that dealt in this kind of thing didn't come cheap.

He might well end up having to ask Richard Baylor for a real job here. And belatedly, it hit him that that would put him and Nic in an entirely different kind of situation. The pressure built in him. He knew what the easiest thing for him to do would be. He also knew he couldn't do it. He couldn't—

An explosive crack of thunder rattled the windows and made his ears ring.

The storm was here. In more ways than one.

He turned back to the autocratic money man and unleashed his own thunder.

Chapter Thirty

N IC SAW THE fancy car leave just after the storm really hit. She half expected to see Jackson in the passenger seat, headed back to his real life. Back to the spotlight, and the fawning adoration of millions. Why wouldn't he? Why would she ever think the simple life they led here would hold him?

Why would she think she could hold him?

She felt a tightening in her gut and a stinging in her eyes as she tried to fight off assuming the worst. She'd done that in the beginning, and he'd proven her wrong in so many ways, yet here she was, wondering if he was on the phone right now, making travel arrangements.

She felt a bit wobbly all of a sudden and walked away from her front window to sink down onto the couch that faced the fireplace. She'd built the fire now, in case the power went out and she needed it for heat, as her father had taught her. As he'd taught her so many other things. Too bad he'd never taught her to deal with a different kind of man than he himself was.

She tried to picture her life going back to the way it was

before, but she had trouble even remembering her day-to-day life before that afternoon when, walking down Main Street, she'd first seen him. Even now, she felt an echo of embarrassment at how she'd misjudged him.

Or had she? Had he been just waiting for this, for them to come looking for him? Was he using his absence as a ploy to maybe get more money out of them? Was it all a plan to keep himself in the entertainment headlines, so his return to the show had even more impact? Was that the reason for the whole thing?

The questions hammered her, countered only by the string of images she summoned up, images of Jackson with Jeremy, the son he so obviously adored. If she had to believe that was a lie, too, that it had all been an act . . . She could believe he'd been acting with her, but if his feelings for that boy were faked, then she was too stupid and blind to be allowed out of the house.

She listened to the rumble of thunder, close enough now to rattle her windows. It matched her mood at the moment. She sat there, watching the fire, listening to the storm, her emotions taking over and making her think that no matter how destructive each force of nature could be, fire and storm, neither could match the way she was feeling right now.

She was almost grateful for the storm, because it kept her from charging up the hill now that the fancy car had left. She wanted to ask what had happened between the two men, and at the same time, desperately didn't want to ask, because she was fearful of the answer.

She didn't want to believe it, but the moment she'd learned that they—that big, amorphous, Hollywood they—had come for him, she'd been hit with the reality of his life, his career. And the feeling she'd never quite been able to fully quash, that this was temporary, just a break, and now that Jeremy was doing better, he'd be back to the bright lights and the fame and fortune, had risen up to swamp her. She'd been afraid of that from the beginning.

It took her a moment to realize the sound she'd heard was not another crack of thunder but a sharp rap on her front door. She knew it wasn't Mom or Dad, because they would have stayed out of the rain and used the adjoining inside door. Her gut knotted, ending her wondering, because she was suddenly certain who was there. And she thought she knew why.

Jackson, come to tell her he was leaving. Going back to his gilded life in L.A.

She yanked the door open, and there he was. Proving her right, her gut yelled.

"Nice of you to at least say goodbye," she ground out to the shadowy figure that made her start to reach for the switch for the porch light.

"Say—What?"

"Enjoy life back in Hollywood."

"I'm not—" She saw him give a shake of his head, then,

vehemently, he growled out, "There's no time for this."

It couldn't have stung more if he'd slapped her. "Fine. Consider me notified."

She had moved to close the door when he said, "Nicole."

Her full name, not Nic. And something in the way he sounded then made her go for that light switch.

She had never seen the Jackson who seemed to materialize in that flood of light. He wasn't just soaking wet, and panting as if he'd run all the way down here, he looked . . . his eyes looked . . .

Terrified. It was the only word she could come up with that fit. Yes, this was a pretty major storm, but they had thunder and lightning in L.A., didn't they? Surely that didn't have him this rattled?

"Jackson?" she whispered.

He sucked in a breath. "I need help, Nic."

"What you need is a towel." She pulled him inside and turned to go get one. But he grabbed her arm before she could even take a step and pulled her back.

"Jeremy's gone," he blurted out.

She stared at him. "Gone? I sent him up to your place when I got back to the barn, so he'd get there before the storm hit."

"He did." Jackson was still breathing hard. "But he hit the middle of the storm inside the house. I heard him on the porch, but I didn't realize it was him. I thought it was the wind again."

"I don't—"

"I think he heard us. Me and Swiff, I mean. The noise came when he was telling me, loudly, that I had to come back or I'd be in legal trouble."

She felt a little shock. She'd barely thought of that, only a passing curiosity if there could be legal ramifications of him walking away. Enough to make him go back? The very thought gave her a chill. But right now, that didn't matter. Only Jeremy mattered, and she fought down a wave of nausea at the thought of the little boy she'd come to love out in this storm.

"Look," Jackson said, sounding desperate now, "all I know for sure is I can't find him. I've looked all around our place, the house, the shed, clearing out back, all of it. Then I came down here, figuring he might be in the barn with Pie, but not only is he not there, neither is Pie."

She shoved aside all the frantic emotions that were battering her, told herself however she felt, Jackson felt a hundred times worse. "Come with me," she said, grabbing her rain slicker and hat as she belted over to the interior door without waiting to see if he followed. She yanked the door open, calling for her father. He must have been in the living room and heard her immediately, because he was there before they even stepped into the adjoining residence. She explained hastily.

"How long ago?" her father asked sharply, looking at Jackson.

"Nearly an hour."

"Should have come to us sooner, boy."

"I never should have come here at all," he ground out between clenched teeth. "I'm not tough enough for this, I'm just a guy who fakes being—"

"You want to stand here blaming yourself or find your boy?" Without waiting for an answer, he called out Mom's name, only to turn and find her already approaching.

"I heard," she said, then looked at Jackson. "We'll find him," she said reassuringly.

"Chuck and Mike are in the bunkhouse. I'll roll them out," Dad said.

"I'll make the calls, get things started," Mom said, spinning her chair around and wheeling quickly toward her computer setup.

Nic nodded. Her father grabbed his own rain jacket, looked frowningly at the drenched Jackson, and pulled another one off the rack. "It'll be a little short on you, but better than nothing."

"We'll start at the barn," Nic said. "The rain will likely have wiped out any tracks, but we might be able to tell what direction they headed out."

She put a hand on his arm and squeezed gently. Then looked at her father. "We'll take the northwest corner." She knew Jeremy liked the grove of pecan trees out that way, because of all the critters that tended to hang out there. "Since there's the road all the way to the fence line, we'll take my truck and check that first, then come back for horses if we need to."

Dad nodded. "The hands will take the southeast and southwest corners. I'll take the northeast."

Mom was already back. "The tree's activated." Jackson looked blank, but she'd explain about the phone tree of Last Stand, a way for a network of locals to reach each other in an emergency, later. "Shane's mounted up and on his way, coming from the north side, and Kane's bringing Lark in their car in case she can help. I spoke to Maggie, and she said Chance got back home this morning, so she'll come with him, and they'll bring one of the dogs that might be useful."

"Let's get," Dad said.

JACKSON WAS REELING. Panic about Jeremy threatened to overwhelm him, so he tried to focus on the information Nic's mom had poured out as he and Nic ran down to the barn. Pie's stall door was still open, and Nic thought to do what he hadn't—check the tack room.

"He didn't saddle him up," she said. "Just the bridle's missing."

Great. He's out there riding bareback?

"Don't worry about that too," Nic said, as if she'd read his thought. "We haven't done a lot of bareback, but we've done some and he's getting the feel of it. And," she added, "we know now he went that way."

She was gesturing toward the far end of the barn, which faced north. "We do?"

"Yes. Because I secured that door from the inside myself, and it's undone now."

He let out a long breath. "Thanks," he said quietly. "For having a brain that's still working, I mean."

She reached up and cupped his cheek, but only said briskly, "Let's go."

They ran back to her place and got into her truck. He would have preferred to drive only because he needed to *do* something, but he knew it would be foolish. She'd grown up on the ranch and knew every inch of it, and he . . . he was just that faker who pretended to be a cowboy in front of a camera.

Finally, because he had to vent some of the roiling emotions inside him, he asked, "Your mother said Shane . . . as in the police chief? He really rolls out just like that?"

"He's not coming as the police chief, he's coming as our neighbor. They're just over the big hill to the west." She shot him a sideways look. "And he always likes a chance to take a horse out and jump a couple of fences."

Jackson's eyes widened, looking out at the pouring rain. "He's riding over, over fences? In this?"

"Saves a half an hour cutting across the neighbors, and nobody in Last Stand is going to deny him permission. Not Shane Highwater."

He knew enough about the man now to know that was likely true. He sure as hell wouldn't want to try to face down the guy who seemed to make heroics a habit.

"And," Nic added before he could ask, "Kane's no soft, studio-type music star. He's had a hell of a life, and he's as tough as he needs to be. And his Lark's a treasure, and I feel stupid because I didn't think of her before, when Jeremy was so . . . withdrawn."

"Why?"

"She used to be a child services officer, but she was too good at it."

He blinked. "Too good?"

"As in, she poured her heart and soul into it, and it ended up eating her alive. So now she works for a local adoption agency. But she hasn't forgotten a thing about dealing with scared kids, so she's coming with Kane."

A flash lit up the sky to the east, and Jackson found himself mentally counting down to the first rumble of thunder, even though he couldn't remember the formula for telling how far away the lightning had been. But even without that, it was too close for comfort.

"She's coming out in a thunderstorm? But . . . she's never even met us."

She gave him another look, but this time it was with a gentle smile. "You're part of Last Stand now. That's all it takes."

He gave a slow, wondering shake of his head. "This

place . . ."

"Yes, it's pretty special."

He lapsed into silence, because he didn't know what to think, let alone what to say. He'd never known this kind of feeling before, this sense of . . . community. He and Tris had always been tight, but that was different. That was family.

Back in L.A., he hadn't even known his neighbors, even before *Stonewall* had launched and they'd been living in that apartment in Burbank. And after, when they'd bought that place with some property around it—a couple of acres didn't mean much here, but it had there—it had been much the same, strangers among strangers. Whether it was ranch life, or simply Texas, he didn't know, but he did know it was utterly, completely different.

And Jeremy had taken to it like he never had anything else. For that alone, he had been ready to risk whatever legal hammer Swiff might bring down on him. But now there was Nic, and he could no more see himself walking away from her than he could see dragging his son away from this place where he'd found such peace and happiness.

Where he himself had so unexpectedly found those things . . . and more. So much more than he'd ever expected.

He didn't know how to feel when their foot-by-foot check of the pecan grove turned up nothing—glad that there was no sign Jeremy had been here, or afraid that he had been and all trace had been wiped out by the heavy rain. But there was no sign of Pie, either, and at least the bright white on the pony would be more visible. Assuming anything would be in this downpour.

This dangerous downpour, he corrected, as another flash lit up the sky. This time the thunder was quicker, sharper, and even to him, obviously closer. And there were people he barely knew, people he hadn't even met, risking themselves out in this, for Jeremy.

When they got back to the barn, there were a couple of new vehicles parked over at the house.

"That's Chance's SUV, with the open horse trailer," Nic said. "He must be already out there. And that's Maggie with Mom on the porch, making more calls. And if Maggie Rafferty calls, the whole town will answer." Jackson felt like he should go over and thank them, but the ticking of time was pounding in his brain. And again, as if she'd read his thought, Nic added, "Time enough to talk later. Let's get mounted up. We'll need to stop by your place and pick up something of Jeremy's for scent, because I'm guessing Chance brought a dog."

In the barn, saddling up her Sass and the ever-willing Shade, he kept glancing at her. There was no hesitation in her, no indication that she was wary of riding out into that storm. Instead, she was gathering up anything that might be useful, from a flashlight to a first aid kit, and loading them into the saddlebags she'd tied on behind her saddle.

And finally, he simply had to grab one of those precious ticking moments.

"Thank you," he said, not even trying to keep the volatile tangle of tension, fear, and gratitude out of his voice.

Nic paused in tightening the cinch and looked at him. "I love him, too, Jackson. Now let's go bring him home."

And in that moment, Jackson Thorpe knew he'd been very wrong about something.

Not only could he love Nicole Baylor, he did.

Chapter Thirty-One

WHEN HER PHONE signaled, Nic realized she should have upped the volume. If it hadn't been for the vibration, she never would have known over the noise of the storm. There was thunder coming from all sides, some a distant rumble with only a lighting of the clouds, some a ferocious crack too close on the heels of a sizzling, jagged streak of pure white across the sky.

She pulled Sass to a halt and yanked it out of her pocket, a little difficult given she'd swear even the inside of the pocket was wet. Once she had it, she saw it was a text from Shane Highwater, and called out to Jackson.

"It's Shane. He didn't find Jeremy yet, but he found Pie."

"Where?" He said it calmly enough, but she was attuned to him now, and heard the undertone of rising tension in his voice.

"Over near the chute."

His jaw tightened. "He likes that spot."

She wasn't surprised. She'd loved it herself as a kid, that little narrowing of the stream just before it reached the sharp-edged drop-off of the small stone plateau. It was only about four feet tall, but it had all the dynamics of a big waterfall, only kid-sized, as her father used to say. The problem was that now, in this storm, the cheerfully flowing, safely shallow stream that crossed the ranch would be a torrent. It would be bigger, faster, and in particular at the chute, quite possibly dangerous if Jeremy got too close or tried to splash in it as she'd often done.

He wheeled Shade around and headed west at a faster pace than she was comfortable with under the circumstances. But the thought of Jeremy out here in this—maybe hurt, if Shane had found Pie roaming loose, although she didn't want to plant that idea—was like a spur jabbing her side, too, and she kept even with him, trusting Sass's steadiness.

They were nearing the chute when she spotted another rider coming in from the north. Another bolt of lightning illuminated the area long enough for her to see the big palomino, and she knew it had to be Chance's Dorado.

She pointed him out to Jackson. "Chance."

"The dog guy?"

"Yes. His horse makes him pretty unmistakable."

"Flashy," Jackson said.

She laughed, making it light intentionally and purposefully. "Yes. We rag on him all the time, such a flashy mount for the unflashiest guy around. But he's a good, solid ranch horse, for all his beauty. And count yourself among the few people who have seen Chance actually wearing a cowboy hat.

He usually sticks to baseball-style caps, like you do. But there's nothing like that full brim in the rain."

She was chattering on purpose, trying to distract him. And in the next flash, she saw him looking at her, and knew he knew that. She also saw the palomino change direction, heading for them. Apparently, Jackson either saw or sensed it, too, because he turned to look.

"Did you see what looks like a big backpack he's wearing?" she asked. "It's something the military uses, if they have to carry their K9s."

"Looks occupied," he said, with a credible effort at matching her tone.

"Yes. He wouldn't want the dog trying to keep up in this. Saves energy for the search."

She couldn't even see him in the darkness between flashes, but she still knew he'd tensed up again. She supposed just the idea of a dog in this search made it that much more real.

By the time Chance pulled the big palomino to a halt, she could see the dog's head over his shoulder. It was almost the same shade as the golden horse.

"Your new boy?" she asked.

The lean, wiry man nodded. "Maverick. My friend had started him in SAR training before he had to leave."

"Oh!" She hadn't known that. "We brought Jeremy's pajamas."

"Good call," Chance said approvingly, and like most who knew the man, his approval truly meant something to her.

"Won't the rain have wiped out any scent?" Jackson asked as she dug the plastic bag they'd put them in out of her saddlebag.

"Depends on how hard it's been raining and how long. Light or short rain can actually help. It's heat and dry that destroys scent the quickest. This has been heavy, but not for too long." He shrugged. "We won't know until we know."

"Here." She handed the bag to the man whose service had put that touch of gray in his dark hair.

Chance took it with a nod and then looked over at Jackson. "We'll find your boy."

He wheeled Dorado around before either of them could answer, and continued in the direction they'd been going. Ten minutes later, they all reined in as they reached the area below the small falls.

"Try yelling for him first," Nic suggested to Jackson.

When he did, Nic drew back slightly at the volume. Clearly, the man knew how to harness the power of his voice, something she guessed he'd had to do in his work on occasion. But it was unleashed now, projected out so boomingly it had her wondering if he'd ever done stage work. And feeling a little silly that she didn't know. But they'd spent most of their time together . . . together. Discovering new things, not lingering on the old.

There was no answer that they could hear. By then, Chance had dismounted, ground-tied Dorado, and freed the dog he'd been lugging from the sling on his back. He opened the plastic bag and held it level with the head of the dog—who appeared to be a golden retriever, not one of the more severe and lethal breeds Chance usually dealt with, and she realized this must be the one Maggie had mentioned.

The dog's head dipped, then he practically buried his nose in the cloth of the pajamas. Chance said something she didn't catch, other than it was in a tone of command. The dog spun around and started off, sniffing fiercely, seemingly at both ground and air. He seemed to be working in a pattern, back and forth before moving forward, along the edge of the now-rushing stream.

They followed a few feet back, to stay out of the dog's way. She noticed Jackson was still searching visually, his head constantly turning as he looked from side to side. When it came to his son, he obviously wasn't putting all his eggs in any one basket. So it was Jackson who spotted the other rider coming toward them from upstream, above the chute.

"Pie," he said, his tone sharp.

She looked up and saw the pony, its markings visible even in the dark of the storm, being led toward them. And the stature and easy grace of the man in the saddle confirmed his identity—Shane Highwater. He was making some sort of hand gesture upstream, and she realized he was making it for Chance, who had probably spotted him long before they had.

"Shane," she said to Jackson. As she said it, the rider

veered slightly away from the stream, away from them. She sensed Jackson's reaction and said quickly, "He must be making sure he doesn't get in the dog's way."

"It looked like they were communicating," he said, his eyes darting from one man to the other.

"No doubt. In whatever cop-to-military sign language there is."

Jackson looked back to where Chance Rafferty was barely visible in the darkness and rain, but the golden dog stood out. And then Shane was there, and she could see the pony was wet, and muddy from hooves almost to knees. But only there, which was a relief. Whatever had happened, he'd kept to his feet.

"Found him just above the chute," Shane said. "He's not hurt, and it doesn't look like he went down." He looked at Jackson. "We'll find your boy. If we haven't in"—he glanced at his watch—"the next thirteen minutes, we'll go to the next stage, which is calling out the full team." He switched his gaze back to Nic. "Maggie and your mom are standing by to make the calls. Sean's already out with your dad, and Elena's ready to open up Valencia's if we need to feed a crew."

She nodded, then glanced at Jackson. He looked a little stunned. And she thought she knew why. "Welcome to Last Stand," she said softly.

Another flash lit the sky. But the thunder rolled this time, not cracked, and the time between told her it wasn't as close as it had been. Then a piercing whistle cut through the night. Shane wheeled his horse around, saying only, "Stay back a little until we know what we've got."

Jackson was already started after him, but Nic repeated Shane's warning. "There's been enough rain that three horses tromping through could cause a problem. I know how you feel, truly, but give Shane time to check."

"Ask the impossible, why don't you?" Jackson muttered. But he reined in a little.

"Why not? You've already done it for me once."

His head snapped around. "Done what?"

"The impossible. You made me fall in love with you."

For an instant, time seemed to freeze. Jackson was just staring at her, and in the next flash of lightning, she saw his expression. It was a tangle, as if he couldn't believe she'd chosen now—which figured, because neither could she—and he wasn't quite sure how to feel about it.

And as they rode on, she wondered if that was because the man in the fancy car had won, and he had decided to go back.

Chapter Thirty-Two

J ACKSON COULDN'T BELIEVE it.

Leave it to Nicole Baylor, the queen of impeccable timing, to hit him with that now. Well, if she'd wanted to distract him from his worry—okay, near panic—about Jeremy, she'd sure as hell done it.

But before he could think of a thing to say, something he should perhaps be grateful for, he heard a string of barks that even the fading roll of the last thunder couldn't drown out. Barks that sounded . . . triumphant. His head snapped around as he tried to pinpoint the direction they'd come from. Another string of barks came, the same number and rhythm, and for a split second, he wondered if the dog had been trained to it. But now he knew the direction and he didn't hesitate. He put his heels to Shade and headed toward the barking.

Another flash, more diffuse now as the storm finally moved away, and he caught a glimpse of movement, up the nearest rise, but low to the ground. A spot of lighter color against the darkness.

The dog.

Heedless of anything now except the need to get to his son, he urged Shade onward. The willing animal slipped once or twice, but recovered. The jolt out of the horse's usual steady gait barely rattled him; he'd been riding on guard for that since they'd left the barn.

He kept his gaze fastened on the spot where he'd seen the golden dog, realized he could now see him even without the aid of nature's electric lights. He saw Chance now, too, crouched down beside the dog.

Visions of Jeremy hurt—or worse—flashed through his mind more searingly than any bolt of lightning. He pulled Shade to a halt and threw himself to the ground, barely remembering to pull the reins up and over the horse's head to ground tie him.

He ran up the rise toward the dog, slipping more than once and not caring. Only when he was just a few yards away could he make out the huddled shape on the ground, with Chance Rafferty kneeling beside it, the dog madly licking the boy's cheek.

"I think he's okay," Chance called out as he straightened. "He found a good place to ride it out, under this stone outcropping."

Jackson flicked a glance and a nod of appreciation and thanks at the man, but he never stopped moving. When he got there, he wanted nothing more than to scoop Jeremy up into his arms, but knew he had to restrain the need until he was positive he wasn't injured.

"You taught me that, Dad," Jeremy said as he went down on his knees beside him. "You said never hide under a tree in a thunderstorm."

Jackson had to think about that for a second, then remembered it had been a line in one of the episodes of *Stonewall*. He didn't let the seven-year-old watch the show, but he might well have heard him going through the lines.

"I don't want to go back," Jeremy said, his voice sounding suspiciously shaky. "I like it *here*."

So he'd been right, he'd heard Swiff giving his ultimatums. "Don't worry about that."

He felt a nudge as the dog again nosed at Jeremy, as if to be sure he was okay.

"Maverick, sit," Chance said. The dog sat instantly, but didn't move away from Jeremy.

"Are you hurt? Did Pie throw you?" Jackson asked, although he seemed as fine as a cold, soaked-to-the-skin kid could be.

"No, he didn't! I'm fine, Dad."

He tried to search the boy for any sign of injury, but couldn't see well enough. And then Nic was there, with a flashlight, kneeling beside them, illuminating things in more ways than one.

"Did you find Pie?" Jeremy asked anxiously. "I tried to hang onto him, but the thunder scared him."

"We've got him," Nic assured the boy. "Shane found him, and he's fine. Just a bit muddy, like you."

She was grinning as if she were as relieved and happy as he was. *I love him too, Jackson . . .*

Jeremy grinned back at her and started to get to his feet. The moment he did, Jackson grabbed him and pulled him into that fierce hug he'd been holding back. He felt almost overwhelmed by everything he was feeling.

"You scared the hel—heck out of me," he said.

"I wasn't scared," Jeremy announced. "Mrs. B told me about what happens here when somebody in Last Stand needs help, how the whole town will turn out to lend a hand."

"Truth," came a deep voice from behind them, and Jackson glanced back to see the Last Stand police chief there, dismounted and with Pie's reins in his hand.

"Pie!" Jeremy shouted and scrambled to get free.

"Guess I'd better call Mom to call off the troops," Nic said, still grinning.

"Already did," Shane said. Then, with a nod at Jeremy, he added, "And I'm thinking the old saw about getting back on your horse might apply here."

Jeremy nodded eagerly.

Breathing more evenly now, Jackson said, "You probably need to thank Maverick there first, though."

The boy immediately turned to the obediently sitting dog and threw his arms around him. "You found me. You really found me," Jeremy said. The golden head lifted as the animal licked his cheek yet again, his tail wagging madly in the mud.

"You're both going to need a bath when you get home," Nic said with a laugh at the face Jeremy made.

"I wish we could keep him," the boy said, then suddenly, as if he'd just remembered, he looked at the man who had brought the dog. "Mr. Chance? Is he the dog your mom told me about? The one she thought maybe I could have?"

"I think," Chance drawled, "he would be now even if he hadn't been before."

Jeremy frowned. "What's that mean?"

"It means that now that he's found you after a search, it'll be ingrained in him to look out for you for the rest of his life."

"I know the feeling," Nic said, just loud enough for Jackson to hear.

I love him too, Jackson . . .

You made me fall in love with you . . .

And in that moment, he knew it was true. And the last barrier to Jackson Thorpe truly believing in what he'd found here crumbled. What had happened here had shown him the truth of this place, this town where strangers would come running to help. He felt a sense of connection, of home, that he'd never really felt before. He wanted to stay in this place, and he wanted the woman who had been with him every step of the way tonight.

He turned to look at her as Jeremy ran over to Pie, more settled now that the storm had moved farther away, and

Shane—the police chief!—gave him a leg up.

"You know that . . . fall you said you took?"

Something in her expression changed, visible even now, in the faint light. "I remember."

"You wanted me to be honest? Well, here goes. I was wrong."

Her brow furrowed. "About what?"

"When I said I'd never be in love again." Her eyes widened. He hastened to finish, to get it said. "I took that fall a while ago, Nic. I love you too."

And at the look she gave him then, Jackson Thorpe had the crazy thought that this storm hadn't just lit up the sky, it had lit up his heart.

Chapter Thirty-Three

"I THINK WE need to make a test run."

Nic blinked. A test run? She had no idea what he meant, but then her thinking was a little foggy after the afternoon encounter they'd just had. The delightful, explosive encounter they'd just had, the latest one in the string that had made the last two weeks pass with lightning speed. She was already regretting that this one had to end before Jeremy finished his session with Mom, and she had to start her last training session of the day with a new client.

"I thought we were way past test runs," she said, running a hand down his back to cup that taut backside she simply loved the feel of. "And we passed with flying colors," she added with a grin.

He smiled back at her, but his voice was quietly serious when he spoke. "I meant a test run to see exactly how long it would take to get from here"—he patted the bed—"in this state, to your folks' house."

She frowned, puzzled now. She slid over onto her side, and he rolled with her, clearly intent on whatever this was. She propped herself up on one elbow. And waited. Jackson reached up and stroked her cheek with the back of his fingers, an oddly gentle move, considering how crazed they had just been, taking each other wildly.

"I know you're worried about your dad," he said. "And you want to be close."

She was no longer surprised when he made one of those perceptive jumps. She'd never told him why she'd always stayed in her wing of the main house, even when this place she loved had been empty.

"Mom can only do so much," she said, admitting it.

"I know. I think if we install an alarm or panic button that registers up here, and we practice a bit, we could get it down to, say, three minutes, to get down there. We can practice up on CPR, too, and I think I could carry him to the car if necessary, and—"

"Jackson," she said, cutting him off. "What, exactly, are you getting at?"

He grimaced. "I just wanted to . . . I'm trying to figure out a way . . ." He let out a clearly exasperated breath, jammed his fingers through his hair, and grimaced again. And when he spoke this time, it was short and blunt. "I want you here. All the time. So I'm trying to figure out how to make it work. So you'll say yes."

"You want me to . . . move in with you?"

"You said you've always loved his place, and I figured the only reason you didn't move in before was your dad, so if I could fix it so we could get there fast enough—"

He stopped suddenly, an odd expression coming over his face. That face millions of women loved, and that she did now, as well, although for entirely different reasons.

"Unless," he began hesitantly, "I'm jumping the gun here. If you don't want—"

She put a finger up to his lips to stop the words. "I want. I so want." She gave him a rather embarrassed smile. "Not saying I don't like sneaking up here while Jeremy's having lessons. It's rather titillating, I have to admit. But things would be a lot easier if . . . we had every night together."

He let out a sigh that sounded so relieved, it made her smile even wider. But then his brow furrowed again. "How would your parents feel about you moving in with me?"

That he was even concerned about that made her throat tighten, but she kept her tone light. "Mom would be delighted. Dad . . . well, he likes you. Respects you. So I think he'd be okay with it."

He looked as if he was about to say something else, but changed his mind. Instead, he pulled her close and kissed her again, long, deep and thorough.

And they nearly didn't finish before Jeremy arrived.

"I UNDERSTAND WHY you got scared," Nic said to Jeremy. "So did I."

The boy looked up at her, some of the hot chocolate he'd

just finished drinking rimming his mouth. "You did?"

"When I found out who came to see your dad, yeah, I did. I was afraid he was going to take you and go back to L.A."

"Me too. That man, he sounded so mean—"

"He did. That's why I told him to get out."

She looked up as Jackson spoke, just as he came to a halt at the table with a second mug for Jeremy. He'd spoken calmly enough, but there was an edge in his voice that made her wish she'd been here to see him tell the guy off.

His boss, essentially. He'd kicked his boss out.

He pulled out the chair on Jeremy's other side and took one of the boy's hands in his. "You're happier here than you've been in a long time."

Jeremy gave him a rather sly look from under lowered lashes. "So are you."

Jackson shifted his gaze to her as he said, "Yes. I am." Nic felt a more searing heat than the hot chocolate flooding her, and she couldn't answer except to hold that gaze.

"Lark says it's okay. To be happy again. That it doesn't mean we love Mom any less."

She felt Jackson go very still before he said, in the tone of a man who felt as if he were walking on eggshells, "Do you think she's right?"

Slowly, the boy nodded. "She asked when Mom was the happiest, and that she bet it was when I was happy."

"She's right."

Jeremy nodded. "So that's why it's okay to be happy." He gave his father a sideways look. "You too."

Jackson's mouth curved into that lopsided half grin she loved. "Thanks," he said, reaching up to tousle the boy's hair.

"So," Jeremy said hesitantly, almost but not quite fearfully, "we're not going back?"

"We are not," his father answered firmly. "We've made more of a home here in six weeks than we ever had in L.A."

"But your boss, he was mad."

"He's not my boss anymore." He gave Nic a sideways look that told her where Jeremy had gotten the knack. "If he's willing to keep on a half-useful hand, your dad is."

Nic couldn't stop the chuckle that escaped. "He'll be willing." *I'll make sure of that.*

Jeremy was eyeing them both now, too young to hide the mental calculating he was doing behind those eyes so like his father's. "Maybe Nic could stay here with us."

Judging by his expression, that had caught Jackson as off guard as it had her. That easily, the task of explaining to the boy was . . . unnecessary.

"I'd like that," Jackson said after a moment. "A lot."

"I would too," she said softly.

"Good," Jeremy said, sounding pleased. He looked at his empty breakfast plate. "'Cuz I like her French toast."

Nic couldn't help it, she burst out laughing. "Then you shall have that treat every Sunday morning."

The boy gave a cheer and grabbed his mug of chocolate, draining it.

She'd swear she could feel Jackson looking at her. And when she looked up, she wasn't surprised; the heat in his gaze fairly sizzled. "And what treat do I get every Sunday morning?"

An answering heat rose in her again. "Oh, I think deciding that will take a lot of . . . experimenting."

"I'm good with that," he said, that rough edge that set her on fire coming into his voice.

As if he hadn't noticed a thing—or as if everything seemed perfectly normal to him—Jeremy asked blithely, "Are we going to get Maverick today? Mr. Chance said we could."

"Then we will," Jackson answered.

"He said his wife was married before, and he was killed in the Army. But now they're married and really, really happy."

Before either of them could react to that, the boy was off and clambering up the ladder to his loft, no doubt to get dressed for the much-anticipated visit to the Rafferty ranch to pick up the golden—in more ways than one—dog.

"Are you sure about this? Staying here with us, I mean?"

She hesitated, then decided to admit it. "You want to know the real reason we hadn't rented this place before? Me. I didn't want to. Because I wanted to live in it. I just couldn't figure out how to tell my folks."

She got that crooked half grin again. Yes, she definitely loved it. Loved him.

"So now you're going to tell them you're moving in . . . with me?"

"Dad'll be surprised. Mom, not a bit." She took a deep breath, then, because she felt she owed it to him, she added, "I finally realized why I fought you so hard, in the beginning. And why I was so quick to think the worst when your boss showed up."

"Why?"

"Because deep down, I knew. That this was it. You were the one. And I was afraid to believe it."

"I'm glad you got over that," he said with that grin again.

She studied him across the table for a moment, taking in every bit of that face she'd come to adore. If he was worried about his current situation, it didn't show. But she felt she needed to know what he—what *they*—would be dealing with, so she asked.

"Are you going to be in big legal trouble?"

He shrugged. "It'll probably cost me a bit."

"And you're really going to walk away from the biggest show around?"

"More now than ever," he said, suddenly very serious. "Because now I know how wrong we were, about so much." He hesitated, then went on. "I told Swiff that too. That if he wanted to move it to the real Texas, instead of some stupid West Coast idea of it, then I'd consider coming back."

"I'm sure the Texas Film Commission would jump at the chance of that," she said.

He shrugged. "I wouldn't bet money on them doing it. Swiff doesn't take well to ultimatums. He's used to giving them. Besides, they've got everything in place back there."

She liked the way he didn't say back home. But that didn't stop her from saying, "Including snow-capped mountains that don't exist. And people driving a half hour outside of Dallas and being in ranch country. Half an hour outside of Dallas is still Dallas."

Her tone was dry, but he still laughed and shook his head. "I know, I know."

"Regrets?"

He winced slightly. "A couple. The crew guys. Tucker, mostly. I think he'll be okay, but . . ."

She wasn't surprised by his words, or that his first concern was that particular group. The one he'd once been part of. She remembered the interview clip she'd come across that night when she'd weakened and done a bit of searching on their new tenant. Tucker Culhane, explaining that Jackson could do most of his own stunts, but didn't so that he, Tucker, would have work.

As she'd predicted, her mother wasn't at all surprised when she'd announced her relocation, after the alert system Jackson had proposed had been built and installed, by local tech wizard, Cody Rafferty. A simple push of a button would set off an alarm in the barn, ranch vehicles, and in the house on the hill.

Somewhat appropriately, she told them on Valentine's Day. She was surprised, and a bit curious, when Jackson had taken her parents aside to speak to them alone for a few minutes. Maybe working out the details of a long-term—permanent, she hoped—rental agreement. But then she guessed she knew what he'd really asked when her mother announced Jeremy would be staying with them tonight, to give them time to get settled together.

She packed up what she thought would be immediately necessary. Jackson blinked at her two boxes of clothes, and a third of boots. "That's it?"

She raised a brow at him. "Expecting a dozen suitcases?"

He laughed. "Guess I haven't completely shed L.A. yet." But then he scanned the boxes and, after a moment, gave her a sideways look that sent a flare of heat through her. "You did pack that little blue number, didn't you?"

"Now why would you ask that?" She kept her tone light, even though her pulse had kicked up a notch.

"Because," he said, his voice taking on that rough note that sent heat rocketing through her yet again, "I want to peel it off you. Like I didn't get to that night after the saloon."

Their first night together. The memories flooded her, and the heat became a firestorm. "I'll put it on the minute we get there," she promised huskily, delighting in the answering heat that lit up those famous eyes of his.

And their first night in their new home together was more than she ever could have wished for. A Valentine's Day she needed no card—although he, and sweetly, Jeremy, had both given her one, along with a box of her favorite chocolate mini-cupcakes from Kolaches—to make special.

Because nothing could be more special than this night alone with the man she'd never expected to find. The man she loved.

And who, beyond doubt or probability, loved her.

Chapter Thirty-Four

H E LOOKED OUT over the rolling hills, a vista he never seemed to tire of. It was obvious why this was one of Nic's favorite spots. It brought a kind of peace he'd never known before coming here. Jeremy seemed to like it, too, because he'd eagerly joined them when they had suggested Pie needed a ride outside of the corral.

His son was coming along so quickly with his riding that Jackson didn't feel the need to watch him every second. Besides, he trusted Nic's uncanny equine instincts to know when trouble might be brewing. As for himself, he just kept an eye out for critters in the brush, or maybe a rattlesnake out sunbathing on a rock, taking in some warmth on this last day of February.

He heard her sigh, and a glance at her very slightly furrowed brow made him ask, "What are you thinking?"

She immediately smiled at him. "Just sour grapes. Very old sour grapes. We used to own from the road all the way out to that outcropping of rock there." She pointed at the rough shape that jutted out of a hill in the distance. He looked from there back toward the road, which was out of sight, but he mentally tried to calculate the distance.

"That'd practically be a ranch in itself."

"Really only a hundred acres or so. Our neighbor, Riley Garrett, bought it when we had to sell something to keep going, because it adjoined her property and, with the connection to our road, gave her access to two exits."

"Seems like a good idea."

"She's a smart woman. And I shouldn't complain. At least she's a friend. She even told us we could buy it back if we were ever in a position to."

The little pinto pony beside them moved, drawing Jackson's gaze. Pie was stretching his nose out to see if any of the scrub within reach was edible. Jeremy immediately patted his mount's neck, looking so content and happy Jackson could barely breathe for a moment. He wondered if he would always be haunted by the silent shadow his little boy had become. He didn't know, but he did know that he would forever be filled with joy at the change that pony, this place, and the woman beside him had wrought. It was as close to a miracle as he'd ever seen in his life and closer than most people ever got. It made him wish everybody who'd gone through the hell he and Jeremy had could find this kind of happiness again.

It wasn't until, after finishing the picnic lunch they'd brought, and they'd mounted up and headed back, that something occurred to him.

"You said that section of land you sold had access to the

road, the same road your gate is on?"

"Yes. The boundary's only about a hundred yards from the gate. Why?"

"Just . . . thinking."

And that night he did some more of that thinking, while they had on one of Jeremy's favorite fantasy movies, with the sarcastic, talking raccoon. Just hearing his son laugh at the on-screen antics had him pondering many things. Including his own absence from that screen.

And how he might better spend his time.

"I NEED TO ask if you'd be willing to do something."

The new tension that had come into Jackson's voice and posture made her reach out and run a finger over the hand that was holding his coffee mug. "Have I said no to anything yet?" she asked huskily.

She'd have sworn she could feel heat shooting through him, as if that slight connection of her finger on his skin was enough. It took a moment for him to go on.

"This is . . . different. Nothing to do with . . . us, really. I mean it is, because we'd both have to work at it, but . . ."

And, she realized, he was having trouble getting it out. She hadn't seen him like this in a while. He'd built not just a home for him and Jeremy here, he'd built a life. He'd put his name on the list for the phone tree, and twice already, had responded when someone had called for help. Once when a car driven by a grandfather with his three toddler grandchildren had broken down a mile away from their gate, and once when one of the wild horses neighboring rancher Jessie McBride rehabbed and found homes for had gotten loose. In fact, it had been Jackson who'd found and wrangled the recalcitrant colt and brought him safely back home. Word had gotten around after that one, and Last Stand had not just accepted but adopted him as one of their own.

She waited patiently until he drew in a deep breath and went on. "I wanted to ask if you'd do what you did for Jeremy for other kids, kids in the same boat. Teach them to ride, I mean, give them something outside their grief and fear to focus on."

She hadn't expected that. "What exactly do you have in mind?"

"A . . . haven of sorts, for bereaved kids." It came in a rush now, telling her just how hard he'd been thinking about this. "I'd buy back the land you sold, so it would have a separate entrance. With an easement for your friend if she wants it, of course. Most of it would revert to the ranch, but we'd keep a few acres down near the road and set it up there, with an office and a small stable and corrals. With your expertise and my name—while it still means anything, at least—to promote it, I think we could do some good."

It was all Nic could do to blink back the moisture in her eyes. How had she ever doubted this man? Because this was who Jackson Thorpe was at the core—a good, decent, caring man . . . who just happened to be the sexiest guy around.

"We could call it Thorpe's Therapy," she said with a grin, despite the urge to cry at the same time. "We'd have to buy some suitable horses, maybe even another pony or two."

"Was that . . . a yes?"

"That was an 'I'd love it.' Almost as much as I love you."

He kissed her then, and it was a long time later that he asked, while lazily stretched out in their bed, "Did you ever wonder what I talked to your folks about that first day you moved in here?"

Surprised, she drew back. "I thought you were . . . arranging things."

"I was. In a way." He propped himself up on one elbow. "I asked them if they'd ever had a wedding up here on this hill." Her breath caught in her throat, but he gave her no chance to react, just went on, as if it were the most casual thing in the world. "Your folks said no, they hadn't."

A whisper was the most she could manage. "And you said?"

He looked at her then, and all the casualness had vanished from his demeanor and voice. "I said, 'Good. We'll be the first.'"

She stared at him, her eyes stinging with moisture. "Yes," she said, putting everything she was feeling into her own voice. "We will be."

He turned then, reached out and gently grasped her

shoulders. "You do know I was never going to leave? I never even considered it. I was worried about how I was going to get disentangled from them, but it never entered my mind that I wasn't going to stay. Here, with you. This is . . . home. The kind I never thought I'd find again."

She enveloped him in the strongest hug she could give. "Welcome to Last Stand, Jackson. You are home now."

JEREMY WIELDED THE big scissors with obvious glee, and with the golden retriever, Maverick, at his heels, headed for the big, red ribbon strung between the new corral and classroom building. Jackson watched his son, overwhelmed by emotion and the tightness in his chest. His son had come so far, thanks to this place, this family, this town. Jeremy—hell, him too—had been hanging on by a thread, and now, three-and-a-half months after making the desperation move to come here to Last Stand, here they were, amid a crowd of townsfolk and visitors alike, cutting the ribbon on Thorpe's Therapy Horses.

The idea he'd broached had met with great success from the beginning, when Nic's friend Riley Garrett insisted on only being paid for the land going back to the ranch; the easement and what he was building was more than enough compensation for the new site.

For one of the few times in his life, he'd been glad of his

fame, glad even for the uproar his departure from the show, now on hiatus, had caused. Not only did they have several kids lined up for the sessions with the horses—which he and Nic had had such fun finding and choosing, gentle, happy creatures with an affinity for short humans—donations were rolling in so fast, they'd had to hire staff just to handle it all. And fronting that staff was the dynamo who one day soon would be his mother-in-law, not in her chair but aboard her horse, taking particular care that the children in sad situations saw how well she rode.

So now here he was, amid a crowd that had accepted him, watching his happy child, standing next to the woman who had brought them both back to life, and all amid the incredible spring explosion of the bluebonnets that carpeted the hills. Last Stand hadn't only accepted him and Jeremy, they had made the launch of this endeavor one of the highlights of the annual Bluebonnet Festival for which the town was famous.

And Tris kept smiling at him, with that *Told ya so* look in her eyes. His sister had been right about this place from the beginning.

He was aware of the looks he was getting, both openly and surreptitiously, but he didn't care. He was beyond content with this life he was building here, he was happier than he'd ever thought he'd be again. And he didn't care how many of the sizeable crowd was here because of who he was. He only cared about the kids clustered around Jeremy as his son proudly introduced them to the horses. Especially the one who'd started it all, Sorry, the horse Jackson had pulled out of the mudflat. And who had, to his surprise, taken perfectly to his new job, that of carefully handling his young riders.

Buck had adapted well to the change also, seeming to be glad to be rid of all the gear and equipment and noise and fuss that being a TV star of sorts brought along. And the selective animal had taken to Nic right away, which, he'd drawled out to her as she stroked the buckskin's neck, pretty much made them family.

Jackson grinned when Maggie Rafferty got up on the platform Nic's mom used for mounting up, which they had temporarily converted to a stage of sorts. Grinned because you could immediately tell the locals from the out-of-towners by who immediately shut up and turned to pay attention, himself included in that latter group. Not only was the woman a force of nature, but her open acceptance of him had hastened his inclusion as a Last Stander.

She spoke first of Last Stand and her love of it, and what made it special. About the mindset it took to really become part of this unique town founded by the survivors of the actual last stand. Then of people who truly fit in, not only because they had the heart and way of thinking necessary, but because they didn't assume they could just roll in and belong.

"Some," she said with a grin, "even have the class not to

wear a cowboy hat because they don't think they've earned it. Including the man behind this marvelous organization we're opening today."

It took him a moment to realize she'd turned it personal. Aimed at him.

"Jackson," she called out, "quit trying to hide over there. Get up here."

He didn't want to, and for a moment, didn't move. Then Nic whispered in his ear, "You know you don't dare ignore Maggie Rafferty."

"I know," he muttered and surrendered.

As he walked through the crowd, applause started, and he felt as if it were something he'd never experienced before. Or maybe it was just because, as with the hat, he'd never felt he deserved it before. But he thought maybe, just maybe, now he'd earned a little of it, at least.

When he got up onto the makeshift stage, Maggie gave him a welcoming hug in front of the entire gathering.

"Well, that ought to seal the deal," he whispered to her. "Thanks."

She laughed, then called out for, of all people, Chief Highwater, who grinned at Jackson as he strolled out and handed Maggie a large box. She removed the lid and lifted out a pristine, dark-blue felt cowboy hat. He'd never seen one quite that color. A memory flashed through his mind, of Nic holding a shirt up to him in Yippee Ki Yay, saying the dark blue matched his eyes and really brought them out. And he knew who was behind this particular choice.

"You've earned this, Jackson," Maggie said, reaching up to plant the hat on his head. "And if anybody says different, you send them to me."

The crowd laughed, and he heard his sister's familiar whoop of support. It gave him a chance to gather his scattered thoughts. Finally, he gave Maggie the hug this time, then looked out at the gathering and said, in his best projecting voice, "Thank you. All of you. This is the best award I've ever gotten."

He meant it, and let it ring in his voice and show on his face. And when he tipped the new hat to the crowd, a roar of approval went up. He saw Nic in the crowd, with Jeremy up on her shoulders so he could see over the other heads, both of them clapping and letting out some Texas-sized yells, and he knew she'd been right.

He was home at last.

The End

If you enjoyed *Making A Texas Cowboy*,
you'll love the other books in…

Home at Last Texas series

Book 1: *Making A Texas Cowboy*

Book 2: *Destined for the Cowboy*
Coming soon!

Available now at your favorite online retailer!

More books by Justine Davis

The Raffertys of Last Stand series

Book 1: *Nothing But Cowboy*
Book 2: *A Texas Christmas Miracle*
Book 3: *Once a Cowboy*
Book 4: *Cowgirl Tough*

Texas Justice series

Book 1: *The Lone Star Lawman*
Book 2: *Lone Star Nights*
Book 3: *A Lone Star Christmas*
Book 4: *Lone Star Reunion*
Book 5: *Lone Star Homecoming*

The Whiskey River series

Book 1: *Whiskey River Rescue*
Book 2: *Whiskey River Runaway*
Book 3: *Whiskey River Rockstar*

Available now at your favorite online retailer!

About the Author

USA Today bestselling author of more than 70 books, (she sold her first ten in less than two years) Justine Davis is a five time winner of the coveted RWA RITA Award, including for being inducted into the RWA Hall of Fame. A fifteen time nominee for RT Book Review awards, she has won four times, received three of their lifetime achievement awards, and had four titles on the magazine's 200 Best of all Time list. Her books have appeared on national best seller lists, including USA Today. She has been featured on CNN, taught at several national and international conferences, and at the UCLA writer's program.

After years of working in law enforcement, and more years doing both, Justine now writes full time. She lives near beautiful Puget Sound in Washington State, peacefully coexisting with deer, bears, a pair of bald eagles, a tailless raccoon, and her beloved '67 Corvette roadster. When she's not writing, taking photographs, or driving said roadster (and yes, it goes very fast) she tends to her knitting. Literally.

Thank you for reading

Making A Texas Cowboy

If you enjoyed this book, you can find more from all our great authors at TulePublishing.com, or from your favorite online retailer.

TULE
PUBLISHING

Printed in Great Britain
by Amazon